LEESA HARKER is
Language and Liter
has been a bank mar
perfume spritzer in
person with the USPC
stories since she was a ~~~~ Red White
and Blue is her first boo

To find out more about Leesa and her work visit
www.leesaharker.com

What the Fans Said

'What can I say? ... After reading the first two chapters
online, I was checking regularly as I couldn't wait for
the next instalment. This is the funniest thing I have
read in a very, very long time. Fantastic writing in the
Belfast vernacular, and cleverly put together. This girl
has so much talent, and should be writing plays, never
mind more of these books. Everyone I know is now
quoting from the book and using the Belfast sayings in
jest. Appealing regardless of your own personal beliefs,
or background, this is genius. Well done Leesa Harker.
I doubt very much this is the last we have seen of you.
Ulster is proud!!'

PADDYPAW

'I work in a factory with mixed friends and every day we
couldn't wait for the next chapter ... it fairly brightened up
a dull nightshift and had us heading to Dunnes for new
chinos ... bring on the book.'

KIERON DUFFY

Fifty Shades
of Red White and Blue

Leesa Harker

·THE·
BLACK
·STAFF·
PRESS

First published in 2012 by Blackstaff Press
4c Heron Wharf
Sydenham Business Park
Belfast BT3 9LE
with the assistance of
The Arts Council of Northern Ireland

Reprinted October 2012

Typeset by CJWT Solutions, St Helens, Merseyside

Printed and bound by CPI Group UK (Ltd), Croydon CR0 4YY

A CIP catalogue for this book is available
from the British Library

ISBN 978 0 85640 905 9

www.leesaharker.com
www.blackstaffpress.com

For my granny, Georgina
(she knew how to tell a story)
and
for my mum, Sandra
(my daily muse)

Contents

1

Mr Red White and Blue Works at le Bru

Well, Big Sally-Ann gat a dose of le clap off Tommy Dick-Fingers last week an sure didden I have to go down til le Bru to do hor friggin back-til-work interview? Here bes me, 'Ack, Sally-Ann, I wonder wud ye?'

An here bes hor, 'Ack, go on, sure I'd do it for you, like.'

So here bes me, 'I'll do it for twenty fegs an a squirt of yer Colleen Rooney perfume?'

An here bes hor, 'Aye, will.'

So I sauntered on down til le Bru stinkin

of le Rooneys an tuck a ticket to get in le queue. Sure le number on le ticket was 29 an ley'd just called number 2 an here's me til myself, ack, I'm gonna be here all friggin day nie in lis sweat-bax. So, I tramped over to sit down an sure wasn't my pink Canverse trainers stickin til le carpet? An lis is me til myself, lis has to be le most woeful place on le planet. Sticky carpet an a faint whiff of Bucky an fegs in le air an le staff luck like ley are suckin lemons, le miserable ganches.

Nen, I sees an auld tramp sittin at le end of my row an sure he's near uncanscious wih le drink an in his hand is a ticket lat says 4 on it. So, lis is me, ack, sure he's near sleepin anyway, sure he's keepin warm in here, he'll nat mind sittin on a while longer. So I gets up an shifts past him an on le way I pluck le ticket outta his hand. Nen he wakes up an is all huffin an shufflin an all – he prabably thinks he's outside le Spar an somebady's nickin his carryout. Nen I says, 'Ye drapped yer ticket, chum.' An sure I passes him le ticket wih le number 29 on an he just smiles an closes his eyes again. So I skips on an sits a couple of rows in front to wait my turn.

Well, sure two wee lawds wih Celtic taps on were eyein me up while I was sittin ler an here's me til myself, sure I'm nat racist, a buck's a buck like. So sure didden I give lem a wink an uncross my legs like yer woman from *Basic Instinct*? Nie, I had pink leggins on but sure didden I say, 'Here luv, no knickers.'

An here bes one of le wee lawds, 'Aye luv, lem leggins are see-through – ye've some bush on ye.'

An ley both bust out laughin an made a pig's arse outta me. Wee friggers. Nen I lucks down an sure didden I put my pink footless tights on lat mornin instead a my leggins an sure le Muff was stickin through le material. It was like a big gay hedgehog. But sure before I cud lamp one of lem wee

3

lawds for their cheek, wasn't Big Sally-Ann called in an sure didden I go on in pretendin to be hor.

Well, yer man doin le interview was like somethin outta le Kays catalogue – tall, dark an bucksome. He had a gorgiz grey suit on, like one ye'd see in Tapman, an a grey silk tie an all. Le most gorgiz green sparkly eyes lat stared through me, settin my flaps on fire. Praper buck material like. So here's me, 'Bout ye, big lawd!' An sure when I went to walk intil le room, didden I trip on my pack of twenty fegs lat I'd drapped in shack an fall intil le room, head first an intil his arms. An sure I tuck a pure redner an he just smiles at me an I'm thinkin, Oh here, he wants intil my knickers big time! An he says til me lat he's fell over before too, an here's me til myself, aye prabably trippin over his big trouser-snake!

Well sure his name was Mr Red, so I said I'd call him Mr Red White and Blue

4

in tribute to le Queen's Jubilee an all, God save hor. So he said okay til lat. Nie he's nat from le Road or nathin. Said he was from up le country, somewhere called Lurgan, but had a flat down le town like. Well sure he was askin me all sorts – when I last worked an what my qualifications were – an sure didden Big Sally-Ann forget to fill me in on le friggin info so sure wasn't I makin it up as I went along? I told him she had a GCSE in knittin an art cos she had stitched Big Darren Bonk-Eye Brown's cheek up wih hor da's fishin wire when he had staggered intil a lamp post after a lack-in in le Tavern. An nen she had helped Mark Pyscho Bates to write graffiti over le front door of some touts in le estate a few years ago. An lat's all I cud think of. But sure Mr Red White and Blue seemed to like it.

He was scribblin down everythin I said an luckin up at me every nie an nen wih lem green twinkly eyes an half-smilin. I think he was, like, mentally undressin me, le dirty baste. If only he knew I went commando his pecker wud be knackin le table from underneath. So sure didden he say I cud stay on le Bru an come back in six months, so here bes me, 'Aye.'

Nen lis is him, 'Good. Hope to see you soon.'

An lis is me, 'Awye.' Nen I uncrossed my legs again an sure didden he just smile an len get up to hold le door for me. An lis is me til myself, nie most wee lawds wud be takin a charge at me wih their flies down after a luck at le Muff through lem leggins. An I says til myself, sure he must be a gay len. An I've enough gay friends, what with our Will, Big Sally-Ann's wee brother, an his gang of Kylie-lovin chums. But sure I cudden stap thinkin about Mr Red White and Blue le rest of le day. His posh wee accent, his grey suit from Tapman an his lovely green eyes.

I cudden even cancentrate when I was

shapliftin a bax a fish fingers outta Iceland an sure I gat caught by le security guard. I had til pramise him I'd meet him out le back of le shap to give him a blowie, but sure didden I do a runner on le dope. Sure he prabably stood ler til midnight waitin for me, le buck eejit. Nen when I gat home, all I cud do was think about Mr Red White and Blue's tallywhacker an his wee half-smile an sure I was moist, so I was.

2

Late-night Shapliftin
at B&Q

Well. Le next day sure wasn't I up at B&Q
doin a bidda late-night shapliftin – a few bits
to sell on one a lem buy an sell sites on le
internet. I had eight screwdrivers down my
tap an a spirit level down le leg of my jeans,
an was just shovin a bax a drill bits intil my
knickers when I saw him. It was Mr Red
White and Blue. He was luckin at me wih my
hand down my kacks an I says til him, 'Lace
knickers, chum. Itch le cratch off ye.' Nen he
just smiles like he knows what I'm on about

an I scoots off in le orr direction. Snared a weaker or wha? Sure I was mortified. Nen I says til myself, ack, I should've talked til him. But ler was somethin about him lat made me nervous. An no man ever made me nervous. So I tells myself til get a grip an goes til luck for him again.

Nen I lifted a bax a 99p nails to buy at le till cos ye have til pay for somethin or ye luck sus, an sure len I sees Mr Red White and Blue again at le self-service till. He was havin a spaz cos it was shoutin at him, 'Unexpected item in the baggage area'. So sure didden I go up til him an say, 'Frig, I've had a few unexpected items in my beggage area chum!' An lat's true, like – Big Billy Scriven tuck a run at me wih a rollin pin one time after he seen in it on a DVD he gat in le shebeen but sure didden he end up wearin it as a hat when I walloped him round le napper wih it. But sure Mr Red White and Blue didden laugh, he just stared at me like I was some millbeg!

An len sure didden I luck at his unexpected beggage an sure wasn't it a rope, a beg of cable-ties an a roll of maskin tape. So here bes me, 'Ye doin some DIY chum?'

An he says, 'Something like that Sally-Ann.'

An here bes me, oh shite he thinks I'm Big Sally-Ann still! So I says, 'Luck here Mr Red White and Blue, my name's Maggie – I was only standin in for Big Sally-Ann yesterday, she gat a bad dose an was in bed all day feelin sarry for herself. Nie don't ye be squealin on hor will ye? Or will I stick lat tape on to your gob to make sure?'

Well, I think he liked lat cos sure didden he tell me to come back down til le Bru to get some extra one-on-one trainin to help me make le most of myself! Says I was a unique character an he wud like to know more about me! Nie I says til myself, I'm nat doin nathin unless I'm gettin paid but len I lucked at his wee arse in lem cream chinos an I says, 'Ack aye will.' So I says I'd meet him outside le Bru le next day an away he went wih his beg of DIY goodies. I had to go back intil le shap cos I forgat to get some sandpaper. I needed to get it to rub off le fake tan lat was stuck to my baps. It's called Fake Bacon an it was buy one, get ten free at le Sunday market. Sure I'd rubbed it all over so I'd be brown for le weekend an when I woke up le next day, it was like I'd dipped my baps in a bucket of muck. An no amount of soap, Fairy liquid or bleach wud take it off. I lucked like lat old doll off *Benidorm*.

Anyway, lat night in bed, I was under my Paris Hilton duvet an cudden stap thinkin about Mr Red White and Blue … his gorgiz green eyes, his wee cute lips an his arse in lem chinos. Sure I was moist all right.

3

Le Red Room of Pain

Well. Sure wasn't Big Sally-Ann ragin when she found out Mr Red White and Blue was after me! Here bes hor, 'Oh Mammy don't start me! He's a cert! An ye're a dirty blirt. Ye'll be ridin him by Monday lunchtime!'

An here bes me, 'Sure you know I will.'

An here bes hor, 'You may get thon minge waxed just in case.'

An here bes me, 'Nie, ye don't call me Maggie Muff for nathin! I'm nat waxin nathin!'

So sure I dandered on down til le Bru anyways for my trainin. But sure Mr Red White and Blue had orr plans an was standin outside le Bru waitin for me. Sure didden he invite me out for a coffee instead! But I says 'Naaaah. Don't drink coffee, chum, but I'll take a pinta Strongbow.' Sure, he says til me, why nat have it back at his flat so here bes me til myself, Oh Mammy I'm gettin rid le night! So I says 'AWYE!'

So he went intil le off licence an I waited outside cos I was barred from ler for drinkin vadki from le battles on le shelf. I'm sure wee Sean le owner wudda let me in but when his wife was ler, no chance. I lucked through le windee an waved at wee Sean. He was all flustered an sweaty, God love him. His wife lucked like she wore le trousers, like. Big manly-luckin woman, like a big German. I don't think she shagged him no more cos I heard he was a three-thrust jobby – sure didden he buck Wee Annie Twelve Toes Maginnis in le storeroom an she told us all about it.

Mr Red White and Blue gat us Strongbow an vadki an sure we wanders back til his flat. Le sexual tension between us was, like, electric. Ler wasn't much said but every nie an again he wud luck at me an smile like he knew he was gonna have me every way he wanted to when he gat me til his flat. An I smiled back wih my best 'buck-me' eyes. Nie I'm nat bummin here but his flat was gorgiz. Big glass windees from floor til ceilin, cream carpets an cream sofas an arty-farty paintins on le wall. He even had a big white piana an all! An a snooker table! Here bes me, 'WHAAAAA?!' Cudden believe it. Here bes me til myself, le Bru's payin ler staff too much lese days. He must be gettin a hundred quid a day to ask people if ley want a job cleanin toilets.

So, I says til him, 'Lis is lovely.' An he tells me to make myself at home. So I kicked off my stilettos an threw my pink leather jacket over le sofa. Nen I caught a glimpse of myself in his full length mirror. An I says til myself, luckin good. I had white skinny jeans on lat

I had tuck a stanley knife til an put rips all down le legs. An my American fleg knickers lat you cud see through le holes on le arse of le jeans. Nen I had my pink boob tube wih le white hearts on. I had gat my hair done by my chum Julie an she had put extensions in so I lucked le part. My hair was near down til my arse. I was like a 'Get 'er Bucked Barbie'.

So Mr Red White and Blue pours us a drink – a vadki cacktail he says – an I thinks he must want me drunk an sure I thought I was gonna melt wih excitement. We gets talkin' on le big cream sofa an le craic was ninety – drink was flowin. After a few of lem cacktails, I was rightly like, an sure I ended up playin 'Le Sash' an all on le piana but he wasn't too happy about me playin 'Don't Bury Me' so I stapped.

Nen I was about to straddle le big lawd when he says, 'Now, Margaret, I want you to know something about me. I like kinky sex.'

An sure here bes me, 'Ack, me too luv. Will

I put my high heels back on? Or will I get on til le piana here? Or do ye wanna do it doggie? But nie I'm nat woofin or nathin like lat!'

Nen he says, 'No, Margaret, come with me to my red room.' Nen here's me, oh frig, I hope he's nat one a lem men who dresses up as a woman or nathin. But sure wasn't le red room for pain? I near died. Ler was a big four-poster bed in le middle wih red satin sheets an a swing comin down from le ceilin beside it. Ler was handcuffs an whips an all sittin' on le bedside table. An nen sure didden I see candles an a carrier beg from B&Q! Nen it clicks an here's me til myself, frig he was buyin lat stuff in B&Q til use on women! An here's me til him, 'Holy bejolie.'

Nie, I'm nat a prude nor nathin – I gat lem pink furry handcuffs at Big Sally-Ann's Ann Summers party an hooked Big Billy Scriven up til my bed. But sure didden he get an itch in his belly an cudden scratch it, an he gat so wound up he farted an nen fallied through on my friggin Paris Hilton duvet! Cont.

So Mr Red White and Blue started to tell me lat he didden want a girlfriend an he liked to whip an slap his 'submissives' an lat he was a 'dominant' an I was thinkin, nobady is gonna slap me about le place. But sure Mr Red White and Blue musta saw my shack an he says nat to worry, we wud have a safe word an if I ever said it, len he wud stap. So I thinks about it for a minute an I says til myself, well, sure ye have to try everythin once. So sure didden I say let le safe word be, 'Ulster says NO!' So sure if he was whippin le tripe oudda me or puttin fegs out on my baps an nen I shouts, 'Ulster Says NO!', he wud stap. So I says, 'Aye, all right will.'

But sure len doesen he say he needs me to sign a cantract! An here's me, 'I'm signin nathin big lawd.' Sure I was scared in case he wud hand me intil le Bru for lyin, or say lat if I was fit for ridin I was fit for work. But he says no, it was part of le deal. An nen I lucked at his wee arse in lem chinos again an here's me, 'Aye, will.' So he says he'd get it drew up for me an nen says I had to go home!

An I was thinkin a jumpin him when he gets my jacket an stilettos an says, 'Until the next time, Margaret.'

An nen I lucked at le rope an le chains an his cheeky smile an I says, 'Til le next time, big lawd.' An I went out intil le street.

Nen I was walkin up through le town an I cudden stap thinkin about Mr Red White and Blue bendin me over his knee an smackin my arse. An sure I was moist enough. I had til go past le affy an when I saw wee Sean in on his own, I went intil see what I cud nab. So, while wee Sean was servin an auld doll, I lifted a battle a vadki off le shelf an slid it intil my beg an sure I was outta ler before ye cud say Smirnaff. So, I sauntered up le road, takin a swig a my vadki an all I cud think about was Mr Red White and Blue an his sexy arse in lem chinos an sure I was soakin.

4

Le BIG Cantract

Well. Sure didden I go back til my flat an ring for Big Sally-Ann an sure she brought hor brother Will round too cos he bes near dead til hear a bitta gassip, like. So I told lem all about what Mr Red White and Blue had said an ley were gobsmacked. Well Big Sally-Ann was – I think Will was expectin somethin even more shackin.

Here bes him, 'Ack for fuck's sake Maggie, I thought it wud be better lan lat! Sure all men wanna bend ler missus over ler knee nie an again, I've done it plenty.'

An lis is me, 'I don't think so chum. I

reckon you're le one gettin slapped up outta you an big Johnny.'

Nen he goes all quiet an says, 'Sure I'm nat seein him no more. He drapped me cos I went til le Kremlin an accidentally snogged le bake off some wee lawd.'

An lis is Big Sally-Ann, 'Ack nie, hie do ye accidentally snog le bake off some wee lawd nie?'

An lis is him, 'We were just dancin and, like, I bumped intil him an le next thing I knew he was on me an lat was lat.'

Nen I says, 'It's lem pappers in ler, ley just make everybady a walkin hornbeg.'

An lis is Will, 'Awye, lat's what I telled Janny but, like, he's havin none a it. Fuck him, his loss, sure.' Nen he cheers up a bit an I'm glad cos I hate seein wee Will sad. He is such a lovely wee kid. Well, he's a kid to me an Big Sally-Ann cos we used til mind him when he was wee. Big Sally-Ann's da thinks it's our fault he's gay cos we used til put make-up on him an learn him dance routines til Five Star an Bros songs in le eighties, but sure it was hangin outta him len. We all knew it.

So, Will starts to tell us about some wee lawd he knew lat was called 'le Sticky Vicky of le gays' an about hie he wanted Will til have a go at makin objects 'disappear'.

'Sure I says til him, "No way, Ho-saay." Sure I'm la founder of le "touchy-feely-no-putty-inny club",' he says. 'An I didden want an arsehole le size of le Westlink underpass, either.'

Nen me an Big Sally-Ann says, 'True, like.'

Nen lis is Will, 'But asides from lat, I'm willin til try anythin else, like. Sure ye don't know if ye will like it, Maggie, til ye try. An if he is as gorgiz in lem chinos as you say, go for it!'

Nen later on, when I was on my own, I gets til thinkin, maybe I shud give Mr Red White and Blue a wee try an see if I cud put up wih him smackin me. So, le next day, I sauntered down til Mr Red White and Blue's flat to see le wee cantract. He was all biz lat I was interested in luckin at it, like, an he said ler were things we cud discuss in it if I wasn't happy, like. So he drapped le contract in front a me an says, 'There you go, Margaret, I'd be so happy if you would sign it for me.'

Nen I says, 'It's Maggie, frig sake!'

Nen he says, 'I will call you Margaret.'

Nen I says, 'I'll call you conty ballix.'

Nen I started to read le contract an here's me, 'Oh Mammy!' Here's what it said.

1) *Margaret will allow me to punish her on a daily basis with as little as a whimper coming from her cutely bitten lip.*

(I thought, dat's nat too bad – sure big Billy Scriven slapped le bake off me after he shit himself on my bed.)

2) *Margaret will eat three meals a day. These will be foods agreed by me. Any*

extra portions will be agreed by me. No junk food or snacking allowed.

(Here's me, happy days, sure hie will he know if I get a pastie bap or nat? An I can spend my Bru money on fegs an fake tan!)

3) *Margaret will only use the 'safe-word' if she wants me to stop.*

(Well, unless it's le Twelfth an nen I'll be shoutin 'Ulster Says NO!' all day.)

4) *Margaret will get waxed regularly and have any other beauty treatments that I want her to have.*

(Here's me, nie no lesbo is puttin hor mitts on my minge – bidda fluff did nobady any harm.)

5) *I will provide clothing expenses for Margaret and choose what she wears and when.*

(Yeehaa! No more shapliftin in Primark!)

6) *Margaret agrees to be whipped, flogged, spanked and to do whatever I say, whenever I say.*

(Here's me, he's a nutcase but he's gorgiz in

lem chinos.)

7) *Margaret declares that she does not suffer from Herpes, Hepatitis or any other* STI.

(Here's me, ack what's a wee dose of VD between friends?)

8) *Margaret will travel to destinations that I decide and I will pay her travel expenses.*

(Lis is me, yeeeooooowwww! Butlins here we come!)

9) *Margaret agrees to be corporally punished for bad behaviour or for my enjoyment.*

(Here's me, oh here, I'm nat gettin my knees done!)

10) *I will not lend Margaret to any other Dominant.*

(Here's me, don't touch what ye can't afford dickwads!)

11) *All sex toys will be kept clean and hygienic.*

(Here's me, here ley don't need cleaned, I have a bath once a week – I'm clean!)

12) *Margaret agrees to caning and paddling without hesitation.*

(Lis is me, ack I used to love a wee paddle in le Pickie Pool in Bangor, like.)

13) *Margaret will not look into the eyes of the Dominant – she will keep her eyes down.*

(Here's me, my eyes are nat movin from lem chinos chum.)

14) *Margaret will go to the gym four times a week.*

(Aye, I wonder wud ye. I'll go an see my Uncle Jim, lat's about it.)

15) *Margaret will not smoke, drink alcohol or take drugs.*

(Lis is me, deal-breaker son.)

16) *Margaret will not touch me unless I say that she can.*

(Lis is me, try an stap me, chum – lem chinos is gettin ripped off ye.)

An nen I was moist again. But sure here's me, I'm nat sure wha to do about lis contract. So I told him I wud have to think about it, like, an he says, 'Take it home Margaret. Read over it and get back to me if you have any questions, which I'm sure you will.' An nen he puts lem eyes on me again an my groins go buck daft.

So, sure I tuck it home to read over it again but sure didden I end up gettin blacked watchin *Dirty Dancin* wih Will. He usually comes round til mine wih le DVD when he gets drapped an we sit an watch it, an he wishes he was Janny Castles wih his snake hips, an I wish I was Baby Houseman wih hor tan skin an thin thighs. An nen by le time it's over, an we have reenacted le last dance on my livin room mat, one or both of us is usually cryin an nen we call it a night. An lat's just what happened lat night so sure I cudden get luckin at le cantract at all.

But sure le next day didden wee Albert le postman rap me up at stupid a'clack wih a package lat I'd to sign for? An here's me, well it's nat a summons cos they're in brown envelopes, so I tuck it. An sure wasn't it a new iPhone? An here's me, oh here I'm like Julia Roberts in *Pretty Woman* an I was imaginin all sorts about me lyin on Mr Red White and Blue's piana, wih a diamond necklace on, gettin le arse rid off me. Nen sure didden he send me a text?

Here's him in le text, 'Well Margaret do you like your phone? I want you to look on the internet at BDSM and look at the things we will be doing in my red room of pain.'

Nen I texts back sayin, 'Dunno about BDSM, but I like a BLT outta le Crusty Bap, like.' So I typed in BDSM to take a luck an here's me, OH HERE! Sure it was men an wimen gettin their balls kicked in left, right an centre – tied up, hangin from le ceilin wih all ler bits on show, gettin whipped, slapped, bit, nipped, spat on, le lat. An lis is me, 'Naaaaaaaaaaa.' So I text Mr Red White and Blue back sayin, 'Yer a fruit an nut chum – Ulster Says NO an so does Maggie Muff.'

Nen later on lat night, I was thinkin about what wee Will said about tryin everythin once an I regretted sayin no til Mr Red White and Blue straight away without even gettin a luck intil lem chinos. An I thought, sure I cud always try it an see if I liked it. Cos I didden think I'd like it when big Billy Scriven wanted til take lem sexy photos of me, but in le end, I loved it! Sure I was writhin around on le bed wih le Muff in le air thinkin I was on 'Belfast's Next Tap Madal' wih hor lat bucked George Clooney– it was all emparrin an all. It's a pity wee Gospel Gail in le chemist wudden develop le pictures, like. Sure when Billy went down til callect lem, she bate him round le head wih hor Bible.

Nen I was thinkin about Mr Red White and Blue's wee arse in lem chinos an his wee smiley lips an all an here's me, Oh Mammy, moist wudden be in it!

5

Maggie Gets le Chinos Off

Well. Sure le next day, wasn't I sittin havin a wee drink of strawberry Concord wih Big Sally-Ann to cheer me up. We were watchin *Columbo* an lat's mine an Big Sally-Ann's favourite programme. Sure we cud sit all day watchin him scutterin about wih his wee cigar an his wee lazy eye an scratchin his forehead an all. I have a bidda a thing for him, but I never telled Big Sally-Ann lat, like. So, we'd been sittin talkin about le cantract an I was tellin hor about Mr Red White and Blue's arse in lem chinos for ages.

An nen sure she was tellin me about le time Big Geordie Miller put clothes pegs on hor nips out his ma's backyard one Eleventh Night, when somebady rings my buzzer. So Big Sally-Ann says she'd answer it an sure doesen she come back intil le room squealin like a nun at a stag do?

Here bes hor, 'Sure Mr Red White and Blue's knackin le door in downstairs, he wants ye!'

An here's me, 'Wha?'

An here's hor, 'Awye'

An here's me, 'Wha?'

An lis is hor, 'Awye'

An here's me, 'Wha?'

An lis is hor, 'Wind yer neck in wud ye?'

An nen sure he comes up til my flat door an knacks! So Big Sally-Ann runs back til le door an lets him in an says, 'See yiz!' an away she runs past him titterin like a wee schoolgirl.

So sure doesen he come in til my flat an

here bes me, 'Nie listen big lawd, didden I tell ye Maggie Muff says NO?'

An sure doesen he say til me, 'Margaret, are you biting your lip? You know that turns me on – I may have to spank you.'

An here bes me, 'Sure I may have til knack yer melt in.' An nen he just laughs at me an comes right up til me til his nose is near touchin mine. He put his hands on my hips an lucked right intil my eyes like he was tellin me somethin but without le words. An nen I go all wabbly an all, an nen he pulls me in an I feels his plug luckin til find my sacket an here's me, OH MAMMY, an nen he smacks le lips on me an I'm tellin ye it was le best lumber I ever had. Well except for lat wee lawd in Turkey, but sure, it turned out he was only fifteen.

Nen I goes til get lem chinos off an he says, 'No, Margaret, don't touch me, only I can touch you.'

So here's me, 'Ack, I wonder wud ye? I've

signed nathin … yet.' So I gives his schlong a tug through le chinos an nen we ends up on le bed! An sure doesen he get his tie an start til wrap it round my wrists. So here bes me an my inner goddess, ack sure it'll be all right, so I goes for it. Sure wasn't I soakin!

So he tied my hands together behind my back an shoved me down on le bed so I was lyin on my hands an trapped. An nen he whipped my Reebak battams an my kaks off in one go an nen he pulled up my tap an sure len out came my baps an sure I felt wick! Light was on an all! An I had sandpapered le baps so much to get le Fake Bacon aff, they lucked like two cheese-tapped scones. Len he tuck my sacks off an he started kissin my toes an all, an I was thinkin frig my feet's rattan, they smell like vinegar an onions! An I've a bunion on my big toe. But he seemed to like it, so sure I thinks, ack aye will just let him len.

So, he kissed me from my wee toe right

up my legs til le tap a my head an sure I cudden move, I had til just lie ler an take it. Nen he did it again an lat time, he spent more time kissin my juicy bits an sure I was beggin him to fill me in quick. An he was just laughin an I thinks til myself, nie, I cud get used til lis, like. Most of le men I'd bucked's idea of foreplay was a quick diddy-grope, or a shacker before ley mounted me. So, I just laid back an tuck it, writhin around on le bed an lickin my lips at him.

Well, sure didden he give it til me for near an hour? Like, Big Billy Scriven only tuck ten mins, an lat included gettin his work boots aff! Sure I was wailin like a banshee … I'm sure old Phil McGrew downstairs was twiddlin his wee sausage listenin til us! An Mr Red White and Blue was so big! Like a tripod. An eye-waterin barge-pole it was. Made Big Billy Scriven's luck like an acorn. Nen sure after we'd finished, Mr Red White and Blue was puttin his shirt on an didden I see all lese red marks on his chest? An I says til him, 'What's lat ler on you? Hope you haven't a dose!'

An he says, 'Ah, no. I'll tell you about those another time. Now I must go. I don't usually do it outside of the red room of pain.'

Nen I says, 'I'll have a red ring of pain in le mornin chum. I'll nat be able til walk for a week!' Nen sure didden he leave me til it, an sure I hadn't even a feg til sit an smoke cos Big Sally-Ann nicked my last pack of duty-free from our last feg run. I was ragin at hor. But len I thought of Mr Red White and Blue an his middle leg an sure I was moist again.

6

A Romantic Dinner an a Revelation

Well, I was walkin like I'd had le skitters for days. Big Sally-Ann gat me forty fegs off Big Neil Chubba Thampson – sure he was only back from a feg run til Benidorm. Sure he was stompin about like le Pied Piper a le Road, wih a trail a skint nicotine addicts behind him, hopin he'd drap a feg or two. Fegs means parr on le Road, like. Me an Big Sally-Ann were hopin til get away on a feg run ourselves if we cud get le money up an I was thinkin about hie we cud get some cash when she tells me lat she tried to buck him an he said, 'Naaaaaah.'

Nen she says til him, 'Will ye nat just gimme a touchy-feely-no-putty-inny?'

An sure he still says, 'Naaaaah,' so sure she was like a batein bear le rest a le week. She doesen like anybady sayin no til hor, like.

Nen I gets a text from Mr Red White and Blue on my new iPhone sayin to come til his flat to talk about le cantract an all! So I says til myself … Right I'm tellin him if he wants me, he'll have to drap le contract, I'm nat gettin bate up by some pervy bastard, even if he is gorgiz in lem chinos. So sure didden I march over til his flat til give it til him. Nen sure he's standin ler wih dinner made for us an all! Nie, we're nat talkin a bucket from KFC or a portion a well-done scallops from Manny's chippy – it was friggin oysters!

An lis is him, 'These are an aphrodisiac Margaret.'

An lis is me, 'Yer what's itchy?'

Nen I wonders if he means lat he's dipped lem in lat date rape stuff an I didden fancy that cos I wanted to remember gettin bucked by le big lawd. Sure big Sally-Ann gat half a le Pride a le Shore band blacked wih hor da's home-brewed patcheen last Eleventh Night, an sure she bucked about ten a lem round le boney an ley never knew nathin about it. Still don't, even til lis day … So I was about to tell Mr Red White and Blue nat til bather wastin it on me cos I was a pure cert, like, when he lifts one a le oysters up an tips it intil his mouth. Sure I near boked – it was like a big snatter. So he tells me to swally lem whole an I says til him, 'I'd rather swally you whole, chum.' But sure didden he give me a tumbler of some fizzy wine an said it was champagne an sure didden it go right til my head, lem bubbles an all, an sure after about ten minutes, I was atein lem oysters like a hungry hoor.

Nen he says til me, 'Margaret, would you

like to come and see the red room of pain again? This time I have laid out some of my toys for you.'

An lis is me, 'Awye will.' So in we saunters an sure I near died. Here's me, 'Whaaaaaa?' Lis is me, 'Lis is like friggin Castlereagh holdin centre in here!' Ler was whips, chains, sticks, metal balls (God knows wat for) an le dildos!! It was like a five-hundred pound bomb had went off in Gresham Street.

Nen he just laughs an tells me to get on le bed. So I lucked at his wee lips an his wee arse in lem chinos an sure I jumped on le bed wih my tongue hangin out like a big thirsty hound.

An lis is me, 'Hie many hoors have ye bucked in here, like?'

An lis is him, 'Only fifteen,' an nen he pushed me on til my front an said to get on all fours, nen he whipped my kaks off an came closer to luck at my arse! I was scundered.

Lis is him, 'You have a lovely bum, Margaret – very soft.'

Lis is me til myself, see if I do an oyster fart nie he's gonna get his eyebrows singed an end up wih a squint! An nen before I cud do anythin le frigger wallaps me across le arse wih le whip! An I shouts, 'Sweet Jeysus Christ le night!' An he whips me again an again. But sure le mad thing was I was drippin. An I thought I'd have slapped le kisser off him for doin lat til me!

Nen he says, 'Call me sir!'

An nen I says, 'Call me "Bell" cos my knickers are ringin here!!' Nen he takes me from behind an goes at me like a barn door in a gale an sure I was lovin it.

Nen after, we were lyin on le big bed an I says til him, 'Why can't I touch you, like?'

An he starts tellin me about his past an hie he was tuck advantage of by an older woman an she was whippin le shite outta him when he was only fifteen!! She was one a his ma an da's mates an she used til buck him behind ler backs. An I thinks til myself, pervy bitch!

An lis is me, 'Frig me, did she put fegs out on your chest?'

An he says til me, 'Oh no, Mrs Robinson loved me, she wouldn't do that.'

An nen it clicked. Here's me, 'WHHHH-HHAAAAAAAAAAAAAAAAAAAAAA?' An he says, 'Yes, but we are just good friends now. She is back with her husband.'

An lis is me, 'Know what it is big lawd? In le words of le gospel accordin til Rihanna, you're fuckin DISTURBIA!'

An I gets dressed an he's all annoyed at me. An lis is me, 'See ye, wudden wanna be ye, big lawd. I'm away.' So I grabs my clothes an runs out til le hallway. I cudden believe it. So, I shoves my clothes on an I runs out an up home. Nen later on, I was lyin on my bed thinkin about him an her in bed – an I was mad wih jealousy! An here's me, oh frig, I think I might love le wee frigger!! Nen I thought about him in lem wee chinos an sure I was ringin again.

A Buck on le Bus Tour

7

A Buck on le Bus Tour

Well. Sure le next day didden Mr Red White and Blue text me sayin to come over an see him cos he wanted to talk til me. So here's me, 'Ack whaddam I doin wih lis wee lawd? He's torturin me!' But len I thought about his wee arse in lem chinos an all, an here's me, 'Oh here, I'm away!' So, I put on my illuminous yella miniskirt an my illuminous orange vest tap lat I gat in Internationale wih a blue suede belt to draw his eye down til le Muff area. I wanted to show him what I had lat Mrs Robinson didden – sex appeal.

So sure didden I go til his flat an he says til me, 'Margaret I want to take you out. On a proper date. A surprise.'

So here's me, 'A date? Where to, like? Sure it's daytime – le shebeen's closed nie.'

An he says, 'Come with me, I have called a taxi for us.'

So we saunters down le stairs an on til le street, an sure hasn't he a fancy taxi waitin, a big silver Merc – nat one from le Road wih feg burns in le back seat an a baldy ex-prisoner drivin it an all. So he takes a blindfold out an wraps it round my eyes an here's me, 'Oh here am I goin for a punishment batein here or wha?'

An he says, 'It's a surprise. No peeking.'

Nen I says, 'Will I hope le surprise isn't me endin up in a wheelie bin, chum!'

But sure le taxi staps nat long after we tuck off an he lifts le blindfold off my eyes an sure we're parked beside le big red Belfast tour bus down le town!

An here's me, 'A Belfast tour? Sure I cud do le friggin tour. My uncle Marty drew half le murals in le estate fuck sake!' But a didden tell him lat Marty spelt 'surrender' wrong on le side a somebady's house an gat his ankle broke for it, like.

An nen he says, 'Trust me Margaret – it will be fun.'

Nen he smiled at me, one a lem wicked smiles an sure I was moist, so I says, 'Awye will, all right. Hoors on tour it is.'

So he pulled me on an winked at Big George who owns le bus an sure Big George said, 'No one else on this tour please, it's a private one.'

Nen here's me, 'Private tour? My ma wud be so proud a me!' I felt dead important, like. An ler was two big fat Americans standin wih cameras round their necks an their faces trippin lem at le bus stap cos they'd to wait on le next bus, so I give lem le fingers on le way past an said, 'See ye – yiz yankers.'

Well. Sure didden Mr Red White and Blue trail me up til le tap, an it was an open tap bus so it was baltic, like. An nen as we drove outta le town he pulls me in beside him on le seat an lumbers le bake off me. An here's me, 'Oh Mammy!!' Sure he near ate me. We were passin le In-Shaps an I cud see people pointin an starin at us like, but sure I loved lat. It was like le time me an Big Sally-Ann were buckin lem wee lads in le sea in Turkey. Sure ler were kids goin past us on lilos an we were goin at it, like. Nen le wee lads' Mas came over an were gonna murder us, so we had to scarper. Sure we didden know ley were only fifteen – ley had chest hair an hard-ons an everythin!

Nen I staps kissin Mr Red White and Blue an says, 'Oh here Mr Red White and Blue, I've never done it on le tap of a bus before, only in le driver's seat an against le side a one!'

Nen he says, 'I'm hard, Margaret, you

biting your lip like that is turning me on so much.'

Nen I says til myself, sure lat's like a red rag til a bull an I opens le zip on his chinos to let le tallywhacker spring out an says, 'Whaddabout a game of Chubby Bunny?' Nen I filled my gob up wih him an he loved it!

So ler we were, drivin past le Waterfront an my head bobbin up an down on his middle leg, an sure here he shouts, 'What's my name?'

An I shouts, 'Soooorrrrrr!' (*Sir*) – will, lat's what it sounded like with my mouth full.

Nen he shouts, 'What's your name?'

An I shouts 'BAAAAAALLLLLLLL, COOOTTTTHHH MM KKKNNOOOCCCRRSSS RRRR RROOONNNGGNNNNNN!' (*Bell, cos my knickers are ringin.*)

An nen, when he's done, he sighs an says, 'Now it's your turn, Margaret.' Nen sure doesen he fling me across le seat, whips up my miniskirt an yanks off my thong, an nen he flings it over le side a le bus.

An I shout, 'My knickers!' But sure he just smiles lat wicked smile a his an grabs me by le hips an pulls up my tap, kissin my baps. Nen I close my eyes an he rides me like le clappers!

An lis is me, 'OH MAMMYYYYYY!' So I'm lyin ler, luckin up at le clouds, wonderin if I'm in heaven an nen I spats two seagulls flyin round in circles over us an here's me til myself, see if one a lem seagulls shits on my baps I'm gonna go ballistic!

Nen after lat we pulls back up at le bus stap an le Yanks are still waitin an ley are even more ragin – an on le way past I says til lem, 'Wouldn't sit on le tap luv, le seats are a bit sticky.' An Mr Red White and Blue laughs an I think, frig I never seen him laugh before, an sure it was so gorgiz I was drippin, an I says til him, 'Mr Red White and Blue, I think I ...'

Nen he says til me, 'Margaret, don't get attached to me, I'm not good as a boyfriend, I hurt people.'

Nen I says, 'I hurt people too, sure I near bit yer todger off goin over lem speed ramps ler.'

An he says, 'Let's go back to the flat and talk more, I don't want to lose you.'

Nen I lucks at him an his green eyes an his smiley mouth an his wee chinos wih le stain on lem an I says, 'Awye will.' Nen I was sittin in le back a le taxi an here's me, 'God's curse lese leather seats, cos I'm slidin all over le joint – I'm soakin!'

8

Back-til-work
Bap Wash

Well. After we gets back til Mr Red White
and Blue's flat, I was so shagged out I near
fell asleep on le bed. Prablam was, I was
afeared a him handcuffin me til somethin
or whippin le melt outta me if I fell asleep,
so I kept one eye open anyway. Nie, I
thought he was in le shawer cos I heard
water runnin an all but len he comes outta
le bathroom an sure he's ballik naked.
An here's me til myself, Jaysus Mary an
Joseph, he's a big buck. He was all sweaty

an all from le steam of le bathroom an his dingle-dangle was danglin like a gooden.

An sure I jumped up to give him a good seein til an he says til me, 'Hold on, Margaret. I want to take a bath with you.'

An here's me, 'A whaaaaaaaaa?'

Nie, I've seen in films an all, all le eejits in le bath together makin love an all an I think til myself, sure lat's nat hie ye bath yerself. It's in, scrub yer bax an nen out. But len I lucks at his wee smiley mouth an his pecs an his big love muscle, an sure I was moist all right. So I says, 'Aye will. But ye have to pramise nat to try an drown me or electrocute me nor nathin all right?' Nen he laughs again an turns to walk back intil le bathroom an le horn overcomes me an I run up behind him like a dog on heat an smack him on le arse cheek, an I says til him, 'Red hand of Ulster for ye, big lawd!' An he laughs again an I think I might wanna have his babies.

Nen I lucked at le bath an my heart sank.

Here's me til myself, oh frig! It was one a lem fancy ones lat lucked like a half a egg, nat attached to le wall nor nathin. An here's me til myself, hie le frig am I gonna fit my big arse an baps in ler wih him in ler too. But sure doesen he start strippin me as I'm standin worryin about causin a tsunami in le bathroom when I get intil lat wee bath.

Nen sure le next minute I'm ballik naked too an lis time I didden feel wick – I was emparred an all. So I does a couple a star jumps so my diddies bounce up an down an sure Mr Red White and Blue thinks lis is, like, amazeballs.

So he gets intil le bath an nen pulls me in an I was sittin in between his legs wih my back til him, an nen he says, 'Margaret, I'm going to wash you now.'

An here's me, 'Wash me? Ack, go on away wih ye.'

An nen he says, 'Just go with the flow.'

An sure he gets a sponge an starts washin

my baps an all, an sure all I wanted to do was burst out laughin – I didden know where til luck! I was gettin my baps washed by Mr Red White and Blue from le Bru! Ley shud give out 'Crisis Bap Washes' or a 'Back-til-work Bap Wash' for dirty horny hoors down in le Bru! Lat wud surely get some of lem off le dole like.

Nen he starts rubbin le soap on le sponge an it's all goin frothy an all, an I has a fair idea of where lat is goin next. Nen I feel a prick in my back an here's me til him, 'Frig, I hope lat's a soap on a rope!' An nen he laughs, an sure doesen he start til wash my Mary wih le soapy sponge! An sure he was goin for it wih le sponge – back an forth, up an down, len around clackwise, len anti-clackwise. Sure le Muff hadn't had a scrub like lat since le mornin after I bucked lat farmer from Omagh down at le Christmas Market at le City Hall. Sure after a barrel of mulled wine, I thought he lucked like Sean Connery an tuck him out le back a le beer tent to get my oats like. But after we'd done, an he stepped out intil le street light, sure he was more like Danny De Vito – I was scundered.

So after Mr Red White and Blue had scrubbed my muff til death, he starts massagin it an here's me, 'What are ye doin down ler? Are ye French-plaitin my muff or what?' An nen I says, 'Did ye scrub Mrs Robinson's fanny, like?'

An nen he says, 'I don't want to talk about the past.' Nen he tells me he'd met up wih hor for lunch an had told hor about me!

Well here's me, 'Are you fuckin touched or wha??' Sure I was ragin! What le frig was he meetin hor for? A cappachinni an a bite of hor pannini? Le dirty baste. But he says lat ley are still friends an all, an sure I was ragin wih jealousy.

An nen he says bathtime is over an I thinks til myself, 'Thank fuck for lat.' An nen he puts his bathrobe on an says he'd rung for a taxi for me an I knew he was pissed off wih me for mentionin Mrs Robinson an I says til him, 'Are ye never gonna let me stay le night?'

An nen he says, 'No, Margaret. I told you, I don't want a girlfriend.' But len sure doesen he say til me, 'Margaret, I am trying. There is one thing that I would like … I would like you to come and meet my parents. It would mean a lot to me.'

An here's me, 'See ye big lawd. Mas don't like me an das wanna buck me – it's nat happenin.' But sure didden he tell me lat ley lived in a big house out in le country – in Lurgan. An lis is me, 'Happy days! Sure auld Lurgan champagne is my favourite drink.' Nen he just lucks at me like I'm nat wise an mutters somehin lat I didn't make out. An nen he draps le bombshell lat he was adopted by lem an he was rescued from his cruel birth ma an all! An lis is me, 'Lat's awful for ye, but I can't go to meet yer ma an da.

Naaaaaaaaaa.'

Nen I thinks til myself, he's doin my loaf in. Doesen want a girl one minute an nen he wants me to meet his ma an da le next! An sure I gets a pure pointy head on an I just walked out to wait on le taxi, an I was ragin, so I was. Didden know if I was comin or goin.

But sure didden Big Sally-Ann phone me when I was in le taxi an says ler was a party in Big Billy Scriven's flat, an to come on over. So sure didden I do a detour an end up ler – an ended up drinkin a two-litre battle a Bucky an sittin on Big Billy's wee joystick of love. But sure didden I feel dead guilty, like, cos while I was bein twirled round on Big Billy's pole, sure I was thinkin of Mr Red White and Blue an sure I was moist.

9

Maggie's Dilemma

Well, le next mornin sure I was havin a
lovely dream about Mr Red White and
Blue. He was givin me a bap massage wih
maple syrup an lickin my nips, an sure I was
Bell again, ding-a-lingin all over my kacks.
But sure didden I wake up to see Big Billy
Scriven sittin against le headboard, smokin
a pipe an starin down at me wih a smug
wee grin on his face. Although, wih le turn
in his eye, it lucked like he was starin at le
wall, which was even more Disturbia. I was
stinkin a Bucky, fegs an sex an le wee bump

in le tartan sheets under big Billy's cratch area made me think he was ready to use me as a spinnin tap again. So I jumped up off le bed, tucked me baps under my arms an run til le bathroom.

Nen I had a quick slash an gat dressed quick. Big Billy was a bit put out like because I had never said no til him before an his good eye was twitchin like mad, an wih le orr one luckin at le wall, well he was no oil paintin. An I thought about Mr Red White and Blue an I says til myself, frig, he's nat lat bad. Yes, he bucked Mrs Robinson, an she knacked ten bells outta him, but his wee arse in lem chinos is amazeballs an his tripod is to die for, an sure his wee smiley face (when he's nat wantin to get me intil his red room of pain) is gorgiz. So I says til myself, fuck it, I'll give le wee frigger one more chance to impress me. I'll go round an get my arse paddled an my nips clamped an see what lem silver balls are all about an nen we'll see what's what.

So I run back til my flat to get washed praper an sure wasn't Big Sally-Ann standin at le door waitin on me. Sure she was black as yer boot from head to toe, hair standin on end, clothes ripped, wih what lucked like blood on hor bake, an she was near cryin. An I thinks til myself, oh frig she's been bate up. An nen I says til myself, ack no, sure she baxed in le Hammer for years – she cud bate up most of le men on le Road. An I says til hor, 'Frig me Sally-Ann, what happened to ye?'

An she says til me, 'Oh Maggie, it was awful, awful I tell ye.'

Nen I says til myself, frig I'm gonna get le long version a lis story, so I brings hor in for a cup a tea wih whiskey in it to calm hor down.

Anyway turns out le head-bin had been mindin le boney in le Estate, an some ballbeg had set it on fire wih hor sittin in le hut inside.

Nie, she wasn't burnt or nathin – she run out when she smelt smoke – but she tried to save it from burnin down, to nat spoil le Eleventh Night, an sure she gat caught in le smoke an all. So sure I had to let hor have a shawer an all. She was more ragin about le boney gettin burnt down lan near gettin kilt herself le big eejit. Apparantly, le firemen had to restrain hor, she was wantin to put le flames out wih hor cardigan. Friggin eejit!

So when she gat outta le shawer I give hor some of my clothes to put on an sure le Fila trackie battams were up hor shin, an le Burberry hoodie was up hor arms an she lucked like somebady outta Purdysburn. So I decides to tell hor all about Mr Red White and Blue an his whips an his red room of pain. So lat tuck hor mind off near gettin burnt alive. An she was all for it. She was oohin an aahin as I was describin le paddles, le cable ties, le big red bed an Mr Red White and Blue's arse in lem chinos. If I had a tenner, I'da bet she was moist.

An nen she says til me, 'An what's le prablam like? Let him slap ye up if he wants, sure aren't ye gettin yer hole every night? An we'll be on le dole for life if ye keep in wih him!'

Nen I says, 'True. But I think I like him more lan lat. I think I wanna have his babies like.'

Nen she says, 'Ack, wind yer neck in. Sure they're cuttin down on benefits nie, yiv to go back til work when le weeans are five – ler's no point in havin' kids nie.'

Nen I says, 'True.'

Nen she says she's goin back til le boney cos ler's a few fellas goin out to nick tyres off cars in le New Lodge to put back intil a new boney, an she's hopin if she rolls some a lem down le road, one of le wee lads will give hor hor hole. So I says, 'Fair dos.'

Nen away she went an I thinks, right – I'm gonna text Mr Red White and Blue an tell him I will go to meet his ma an da le marra. Sure what harm can it do? An like, nobady had ever wanted me to meet their ma an da ever. Like, one time Big Billy Scriven's ma came til his flat to clean, an do his washin, an sure hadden I been gettin it hard up against le wardrobe at le time. Sure he hid me under le bed an sure I was ballik naked. Le auld doll was ler for over an hour, hooverin an cleanin. An I was stuck in a twisted heap under his bed wih his ashtrays an used condoms. Sure I ended up wih a dead leg an feg ash stuck til my baps – sure his flat was stinkin like. In le end I just gat out from under le bed an says til hor, 'Sarry luv, luck away til I get my clothes on.' Sure she didden take hor eyes off my baps le whole time, le big lesbo. An nen she started slappin le bake off Big Billy, so I bolted out le door.

An lat's le only time I ever met somebady's ma. An ler was Mr Red White and Blue actually invitin me! Le shack! Nen I thinks, sure if they're dicks sure I can luck to see what dear stuff they have an give their address on til Big Bruce 'Le Housebreaker' an he'll gimme a tenner for it.

So I puts in le text, 'Rite, I've changed my mind I'll go til yer ma an da's 2mara. Pick me up at lunchtime an wear dem chinos. ☺'

Nen he replies, 'Great. We will have fun. Bring a bathing suit – they have a jacuzzi in the outhouse.'

Nen I says til myself, a Jacuzzi in le outhouse? Whaaaaaa? Ley must be minted like! So I grabs my Katie Price bikini lat gets me wolf-whistles at le beach in Benidorm – le diamante one – an slaps some Fake Bacon on til my baps an here's me til myself, floozy in le jacuzzi here we come!

10

Meetin le Parents

Well. Sure le next day, we gat le train down til Lurgan. I thought it wudda tuck hours but sure it was only half an hour. I decided til dress down lat day, wih meetin le ma an da an all, but I wanted to still be Maggie Muff – just a swanky version. So I decided to go commando – no bra, no knickers – sure Mr Red White and Blue would love it. I was beginnin to like playin wee games wih him, especially ones where I had le upper hand. I wore my blue denim skirt lat I gat in Tammy Girl in 1996 an my white knee boots lat Big Sally-Ann shaplifted from Tapshap for my birthday. Nen I puts on my new white furry jumper lat I gat at le Sunday market. It was five quid, like – dear for up ler – but it was so fluffy, an if Mr Red White and Blue groped my baps through it, which I was sure he wud, they'd feel like two big marshmallas. An le rules says if yer legs are out, keep yer baps in an vice versa, unless it's a lack-in at le shebeen an nen it's everythin out an shake it all about!

Well, on le train, I was regrettin le no-bra idea. Le material in my new tap felt like it was made from fibreglass an it was aggravatin my baps so much, my nips were stickin out like JCB starter buttons. I was itchin an pullin an tryin to poke lem back in again. Mr Red White and Blue thought lis was a geg, like. He was sittin facin me, starin at my baps jigglin about le place.

Nen I was gettin nervous a bit about meetin his ma an all, an he says til me,

'Margaret, stop biting your lip – you know how it makes me hard.'

Nen I just decides to give him a wee taster of whats to come after our meetin wih his ma an da, an I gives him a sexy wink wih my right eye. An he just smiles at me so I winks wih my orr eye an he smiles again. So I shoves my feet up either side of him on le seat an winks wih my 'special' eye an sure his face is a picture – shack or whaaaaa?

Nen I says til him, 'Whaddabout a quickie in le bogs like?' So we shuffled down le train til we gat ler an sure wasn't it like an upright coffin. Le size of it! But sure I slid in an whipped my skirt up to reveal le Muff, an sure didden his eyes near pap out. So he squeezed in too an lacked le wee door. Sure we were like two horny sardines. Nen he shifts me up on til le sink an flaps out le tripod. An sure wih le vision of thon beast stickin outta his chinos an le bumpin of le train, sure I was soakin.

So sure he wings his train intil my tunnel an my arse is near fillin le wee sink lat I'm sittin on. Nen just as I was thinkin, I hope lis thing doesen collapse, sure my arse cheek shifts an turns le tap on. So I'm gettin rid from one end an splashed from le orr end. An nen I fling my arm out to steady myself an I turn on le hand-dryer. So sure at least le noise of lat drowned out my yells. So after he finishes, he gets cleaned up an zipped up, an nen he lucks at me an sure I says til him, 'S'all right, I'll just drip-dry, chum.' An sure I know he wants me again but len we're pullin intil Lurgan station an we have to go. So we gets off le train an intil a taxi, an sure I bit my lip le whole way til his ma an da's house, just to wind him up.

Nen we gets ler an here's me, Whaaaaaaaaaaaaaaa? It was like somethin outta *Cribs* – all big an cream wih hangin baskets an a welcome mat. I was expectin Mariah Carey to waltz down le steps in a thong an high-heels at any minute. Nat le kinda place ye drap yer feg ash, or tramp dog shite intil le carpet, like. Nen we goes inside an isn't le hallway even bigger lan my whole flat? Lers a big fancy staircase an marble floors an I thinks til myself, holy shit, we aren't in Kansas nie!

Nen doesen his ma come down le stairs dressed like Joan Collins in *Dynasty* an she comes right up til me, shakes my hand an says, 'Margaret. Lovely to meet you.'

An I thinks til myself, if you knew where lat hand was ten minutes ago luv, ye wudden be touchin it. But I just says, 'Awye.' Nen I sees hor luckin at my baps an I lucks down an sure I says til myself, oh frig lem nips is like two upside down pokes nie. Nen sure doesen le da come in an nen sure I knows where Mr Red White and Blue gets his lucks from. He's a bit like a James Bond. Nen I thinks til myself, Nie I wudden mind a sandwich wih junior at one end, senior at le orr end, an me in le middle. Le name's Red. Red White and Blue. Double-dick-heaven. An nen, like any man wud, he zooms intil le baps an I'm sure he had a semi. So we shakes hands an I bit my lip at him, but he didden jump on me or nathin an nen I lucks at Mr Red White and Blue an sure he's pure ragin!

So his ma takes us intil le dinin room an sure it's like le Mad Hatter's tea party – buns, cakes, teapats, triangle sandwiches wih le crusts aff, le lat. Nie, goin for tea in my ma's house is a tatey-crisp sandwich or a bidda buttered crusty bap, an a feg an a diamond bun from le bakery for afters. So I gets stuck intil le grub while gettin questioned by lem all. Mr Red White and Blue senior asks me about my 'parents' an I tell him lat my ma lives up le Shankill Road, near til le stadium. Nen he asks me what my da does for a livin an I says til him, 'He died when I was a wee girl.' But I never mentioned le fact lat my ma wasn't a hunderd percent sure who my da actually was. She just used to say, 'Le seventies were a bidda a blur, luv, sure I can't remember everythin.'

I cud see Mr Red White and Blue squirmin a bit when I was gettin le Spanish Inquisition off his ma an da an I realises hie different we actually are. Like from different worlds, an lat made me a bit sad. Nen, Mrs Red White and Blue asks me what I do for a livin an I says til hor I'm on a career break (I heard some swank sayin lat in le Bru one day) an she is about til ask me more when she staps dead an glares at me – sure I was only dippin a mini chocolate muffin intil my cuppa tea. She was pure disgusted! Like I was an inbred or somethin. An I'm nat – my ma told me it was all rumours about hor an my Uncle Marty.

Nen Mr Red White and Blue senior asks me where I gat my 'rather fetching' tap, an sure I tells him about le wee prablam wih my nips gettin scuffed to bits an sure doesen he start laughin an go intil a coughin fit, an Mrs Red White and Blue has to get up an slap him on le back to get him to stap. Nen he staps coughin an sure she keeps on whackin le poor shite anyway.

Nen Mr Red White and Blue junior says maybe he should show me around le place an his ma an da says they will leave us til it. I think Mrs Red White and Blue was glad to see le back of us. So I says, 'Awye, will.'

11

Floozie in le Jacuzzi

So sure we gets outside an ler is le wee
outhouse wih le jacuzzi in it. I run over til
it an sure here's me, 'Whaaaaaaaa?' Mr Red
White and Blue presses a button lat turns it
on an it starts bubblin away. It was far better
lan le Shankill swimmers wave machine, like.
So Mr Red White and Blue says he's away
to get his trunks, an tells me to get changed
in le cubicle beside le jacuzzi. So sure I slips
intil my pink diamante Katie Price bikini lat
I gat on ebay, an runs out til le jacuzzi so I'd
be le first one in. Nen I whacks le baddams
off an when I see Mr Red White and Blue

comin across le garden, I flung lem out le door at his head.

He laughs but len he lucks cross an says, 'Now, Margaret, I will have to punish you later for your bad behaviour.'

An I says til him, 'Bring it on big lawd.' Like, I didden know where I was gettin le bravery from cos I sure didden want a wallopin – or did I? I think it musta been le country air makin me a halfwit or somethin.

So, sure he gets intil le jacuzzi an sure doesen he have two glasses a lat champagne again in his hands. An here's me, 'Bubbly in le bubbles – nie I know I'm wih le swanks in Lurgan.' So, we start gluggin. But sure, after scoffin down all lem buns an all, an nen le bubbly on tap, I feels wind buildin up in my belly. Ye know hie if ye luck at a water tap ye need to have a slash? Well le bubbles in le jacuzzi had lat effect on my arse. An I knew it wudden be a wee poof. We're talkin thunder farts, like carpet gettin ripped up. But len

I thinks, sure my arse is under water, sure he'll nat know if I'm trumpin like a farmer or nat. So, I let rip. But instead of it bubblin out le back, a rumble of farts went right up le front of le Muff an bubbled til le tap, just as Mr Red White and Blue leaned in for a kiss. An what I hadn't accounted for was le smell. When le fart bubbles papped at le surface, le smell was putrid. An right in Mr Red White and Blue's face. An nen sure his nose started twitchin an he stapped kissin me, an lis is me til myself, Oh here I'm drapped nie, like. But sure, he wasn't bathered. Next thing he was playin le hairy banjo on le Muff under le water. Nen sure I says til him, 'Whadda bout a wee game of underwater nob-gobblin?' An he nods an leans back on le side a le Jacuzzi, so under le water I goes for a tune on his flute. But sure didden I near drown after a few blows an I had til come up for air. But sure it was just as well cos Mr Red White and Blue senior was danderin across le garden in his Speedos to join us.

Nen here's me, 'Oh frig, I'm naked under le water.'

An Mr Red White and Blue says, 'That'll teach you, Margaret.'

Nen sure I takes a pure beamer cos as Mr Red White and Blue senior's steppin in, he lucks down an I'm sure he's thinkin til himself, either ler's an otter in our Jacuzzi or young Margaret's in le nudie an isn't friends wih hor razor. But sure we has another few glasses of champagne an sure I forgets all about it. Nen Mr Red White and Blue junior says it's time to go, an he gets out. An I luck at him as if to say, 'Your da's gonna get a face full of bush if I've to squeeze past him in le nip here,' so he lifts my pink thong an flings it intil le Jacuzzi an I sticks it on.

Nen Mr Red White and Blue senior laughs an says, 'You are a naughty one, Margaret.'

An sure I take a pure redner when I'm steppin out. Nen I thinks til myself, sure Big Billy Scriven's nat much younger lan him, so I give my diddies a quick shake in his face just for le craic. Sure I cud still hear him laughin when we were goin out le front door til le taxi.

So on le train on le way back, Mr Red White and Blue is dead quiet again an I think maybe I overdid it wih le shakin le diddies at his da an le fanny-farts an all. So I asks him will he come back til my flat to stay le night, an sure he says no an my wee heart breaks. So he gets me a black taxi at le train station and, as I drive away, I try one more time an flash my baps at him through le windee. But he just waves at me. So I sit back in le seat an feel so sad.

Nen le taxi driver says, 'Put lem diddies away luv or I'll be runnin us intil a wall here.'

So I pull my tap back down an nen I sits an tells him all about Mr Red White and

Blue. Le whole story from our meetin at le Bru, til my nips gettin abused by my new tap. So, after ages sittin outside my flat, he finally lets me go. Sure, he thought he was on til a winner wih le meter tickin while I told him my troubles, but sure le twenty pound note I give him was a pure fake, so I gat six quid change back intil le bargain. Result!

Nen I gets intil my flat an sure I was so depressed about Mr Red White and Blue nat wantin to spend le night wih me, I rings Big Sally-Ann to tell hor. I told hor about Mr Red White and Blue's ma an da's house an le jacuzzi an all an she said it all sounded too good til be true. Nen I tells hor about Mr Red White and Blue nat wantin me to touch him an lat he wudden stay wih me an lat I was lonely, an she says lat's nat on like. So she ends up comin round to have a sleepover at my flat wih me, an sure didden she bring hor *Columbo* baxset, an a battle of gin lat she nicked off hor da. An sure, lis is me, my boy might be a rare bear but my best mate is le dogs ballix like.

12

Nine-til-five Hell

Well, le next day, I woke up tap-an-tailed wih Big Sally-Ann. An lat's worse lan it sounds, cos hor feet are le size a breeze blacks, an ley smell of cheese an sweat. An sure she is le length of le bed, so lem kebs were restin on my pilla right beside my head. It was like bein brought round wih smellin salts. So I gat up to make us a bacon sandwich when I heard my phone beepin.

Sure it was Mr Red White and Blue sendin me a text message an here's what it says, 'Margaret, you are going to get a phonecall from the Bru. Don't be alarmed; it's nothing to do with me. You have just been selected, along with a few others, to go on a trial work placement in Tesco. I'll try to get you off because I need you to save all your energy for me. Just go along with it for now.'

So here's my text back, 'Ye'd better get me off big lawd, I'm nat standin up ler packin begs for grannies lat stink of pish.'

So later lat day, I gat le call an had to report to le Bru le fallowin day or my dole wud be stapped. But le best thing was, Big Sally-Ann had been called in too, so it wasn't too bad – at least I had company – an off we tratted til le Bru. Sure we were ragin havin to get up at eight a'clack. Lat's still le middle a le night for us, like. Especially cos Big Sally-Ann sits up til le wee hours watchin *Prisoner Cell Block H* reruns. I think she secretly has a crush on some of lem prisoner women, like, but I never said nathin til hor about it. So we gets down til le Bru an Mr Red White and Blue's ler, luckin all shifty an all.

An I thinks til myself, somethin's nat right here. So we all gets called in separate to get spoke til about our work placements. I gat some skinny, flat-chested bitch lat was half-washed luckin. Sure she was sittin talkin down til me like I was some kinda peasant. But sure I just says, 'Awye,' in le right places, an I cud tell she wanted a rise outta me but sure I was still in lat dreamy after-sex phase where ye don't give a frig about nathin. Nen when I gets out, Mr Red White and Blue drags me intil a corner an I thinks til myself, oh here, he wants me in le Bru. Nie, it wudden be le first time. Sure I bucked le wee security guard in le back corner behind le phonebax so he cud put me til le front of le queue one time.

But, no, it wasn't a buck Mr Red White and Blue was after. Sure didden he tell me lat le flat-chested freak, Deirdre, was his ex an she was out to get me cos she was mad wih jealousy! An here's me, 'I'll knack hor melt in right nie!' But Mr Red White and Blue says lat's what she wanted so I cud get put off le Bru. She wanted to hit me where it hurt. Sure I was like a batein bear. But Mr Red White and Blue pramised to sort hor out an in le meantime sure I had to go up to Tesco wih a bunch of dicks an work. Actually work! So I went outside to have a feg an told Big Sally-Ann all about it. Sure she was as ragin as me. She was wantin to ring Deirdre's neck but len le minibus pulled up for us an she gat sight of le driver an it was lust at first sight – for hor anyway. His name was Igor an he was from Transylvania. She sat up front wih him talkin while I sat at le back wih le wee millies. Sure they were all from le Antrim Road an were wee greeners, but lat didden bather me, we were all in it tagether – it was us against le Bru. Ler were plans discussed about contaminatin food, spillin milk on floor so le customers wud slip, an orr things to make Tesco sack us all on le first day. Sinead was le one who put herself forward as le leader an hor sidekick Donna was eggin hor on.

So we all gat intil Tesco an Big Sally-Ann swapped numbers wih Igor an nen he left an said he'd be back to pick us up at five a'clack. A whole eight hours to spend in a shap! I felt sick. So Sinead an Donna gat to work causin havoc right away but sure didden I get stuck in le storeroom checkin lat none of le eggs in baxes were cracked. Well, after about half an hour, I gat bored of le eggs, an Sinead an Donna had been tuck off le floor an sent to pack begs cos of their bad behaviour. I heard le manager screamin about wafer-thin ham put in baxes a cornflakes, an Sinead pole-dancin round a fresh baguette. So I decided to text Mr Red White and Blue. I started wih a cheeky one sayin I was bitin my lip, an one thing led to another an I ended up sex-textin him. Nie, I was a pro at lis. Sure didden me an Big Sally-Ann work on one of lem sex chat-lines for a while. So I knew hie to get a man from flap to splat in minutes. Prablam was, ye had to keep le men on la phone for as long as passible to get le money off lem, so we gat sacked. Too sexy for le job. An it was workin a treat on Mr Red White and Blue. I was tellin him about me havin a fiddle in le storeroom, an he was tellin me about him havin a fiddle under his desk at le Bru. But len sure didden he want me to text him pictures? An here's me til myself, oh frig I forgat I had a fancy phone nie lat tuck pictures an all.

So I takes le kacks off an sets a few eggs on le floor, len squats over lem so le Muff's on show.

Nen I takes le pic an sends it wih a note sayin, 'Luck what I've laid ... hope it's you I'm layin later big lawd.'

Nen he texts back, 'You are naughty, Margaret. I may have to spank you later. One more pic and make it a good one.'

So sure I was about to do somethin filthy wih a battle a Cillit Bang when sure in walks le manager wih Sinead an Donna. An sure I'm still squatted over le eggs on le floor.

Le manager lucks shacked, but Sinead just busts out laughin an says, 'Fuck me, it's le Easter Hun-ey!' an Donna is in a wrinkle.

An I says til lem, 'Just keepin le eggs warm, all part of le service, chum.'

An nen le manager starts yellin an shoutin at us, an sure le three of us are in a pure fit of laughs. So he rings down til le Bru an gets lem to send le bus up for us. But Big Sally-Ann is nowhere to be found. Nen, Igor arrives an sure Big Sally-Ann is already on le bus, an I can tell from hor rosy cheeks an le state of hor hair lat she's somehie sneaked out a Tesco an has been buckin Igor. So I high-fives hor an we head back til le Bru.

Well, Deirdre-No-Diddies is pure ragin when she sees us back. Mr Red White and Blue winks at me as we are told nat to come back to work an lat we are bein kept on le Bru for nie. Me an Sinead swap numbers an say we'll meet up again, maybe down le town for a wee night out, an I wish she lived on our side of le Road cos she's great craic like. But lat's just le way it is. Nen, as we're leavin, Mr Red White and Blue gives me a cheeky nip on le arse an whispers, 'See you later, sexy.' An sure I walks outta ler drippin like a water tap.

13

Doggin in Duncrue

Well. Big Sally-Ann is a dark horse. Sure hor an Igor were down in Duncrue doggin while me, Sinead an Donna were workin hard in Tesco! I cudden believe it. She told me all about it back at my flat later lat day. He had told hor to go intil Tesco an nen say she was on hor moons an had to go til le bog, an nen he wud be waitin for hor at le fire exit. Nie, I thought til myself, here, he's done lis before, but I didden wanna spoil Big Sally-Ann's ride – she seemed to really like Igor. So sure he picked hor up from le fire exit an tuck hor over til Duncrue. Nen he parked down some road where all le trucks an all were. Nen she says ley were like wild animals, rippin each orr's clothes off an makin love on all le seats of le bus. And, yes, she said, 'makin love'. Nen, he trailed hor off le bus an had hor up against le side of it. She had told him to watch in case ley were caught, but he said it added to le thrill an she just went wih it!

She said Igor was huge too. As big as Long Schlong Silver, le stripper lat we saw in Benidorm last year. Sure he had gat Big Sally-Ann up on til le stage an made hor slap sun-cream all over his wilbert. An I think his plan was to swing it about an flick le sun-cream all over hor. But sure before you cud say 'factor fifty', she was squirtin le cream all over him. An sure he near died – it was in his long hair, in his eyes an everythin. She's mustard when she gets started, like. In le end, a bouncer had to pluck hor off him an we told nat to go back til lat bar. Sure yer man was cryin an all. Well, it was his own fault – lat's what ye get for pickin on a quiet-luckin one.

But sure le sight of Big Sally-Ann gettin thrust up le side of a minibus attracted le attention of le truckers an before ley knew it, ler was a crowd gatherin so Igor tuck hor back intil le bus to save hor madesty. An Big Sally-Ann was laid out on le aisle of le bus, gettin le ride of hor life from Igor an when she was just about to explode intil a million pieces wih orgasmic glee, instead of shoutin, 'Oh Igor!' like a normal person, le eejit shouts, 'YOUUUUU RAAAANNGGGGGG?' in hor best Transylvanian accent. Sure hor biggest fantasy is gettin bucked an bit on le neck by Dracula. An big Igor is as close as she'll ever get til lat. Like Dracula's wee brother – a bit less sexy, an a bit less cunning, but still buckable. But she said like after ley were done, he was all romantic an all an tuck hor intil le Portside Inn for a pint an a prawn sandwich.

An I says til hor, 'True love, Sally-Ann. Will I buy a hat?'

Nen she says, 'Ack, no. He's only here temporary sure. He's to go back to Transylvania soon.'

Nen I feels sarry for hor cos she's never really liked a man before. She only just bucked lem for le sake of it. Nen she gat a wee text from Igor an sure hor face lit up an I thinks til myself, nie he may like a bidda outdoorsy sex an he's probably gonna get lifted back til Transylvania soon, but I was dead happy for Big Sally-Ann. Nen as she was textin back an gigglin til horself, I thought about my man, Mr Red White and Blue. I cudden believe lat me an Big Sally-Ann actually had boyfriends, even though mine wanted to whip le tripe outta me an hors was intil doggin. Mr Red White and Blue had said he'd be spankin me later lat night an I was ready for it. I was thinkin I was gonna answer le door til him butt-naked an bendin over – a vertical smile to greet him.

So, after Big Sally-Ann went, I gat up to tidy le place. I washed my Paris Hilton bedsheets (I had til, cos ley were about to crack in le middle) an nen I hoovered, dusted, palished an emptied le ashtrays, all ten of lem. Nen I gat to luck at myself in le mirra, an I says til myself, nie your turn, so I had a bath. An lat's somethin I never do durin le week – I have a bath every Saturday, whether I need it or nat. But I wanted to be nice an fresh for gettin a hidin off my boyfriend lat night. I thought about gettin a wax but le wee salon on le Road was full a Barbie dolls an I didden want lem gawkin at le Muff, an besides, it was like a wee pet til me nie. I cudden get rid of it just like lat. My muff's for life, nat just for Christmas. So I put on a black dress lat ye cud see my arse in when I bended over, an red lipstick lat I nicked in le chemist an sure I was buckalicious.

So, I tuck a drap a vadki to help wih le pain I was about to get, an I sat an waited on Mr Red White and Blue, my arse twitchin at le thought of what was to come. An sure I was ding-a-lingin all right.

14

Music til My Ears

Well. Sure didden Mr Red White and Blue text to say he was sendin a taxi for me an I was to go to his flat instead. Sure I was a bit put out, like, after all le cleanin an all lat I'd done especially for him. But len I rang Big Sally-Ann an told hor if she wanted to, she cud bring Igor intil my flat an buck him ler, cos lyin on cancrete an all in le street gives ye piles, like. So sure she was all biz an pramised to clean all le jiz up an all, so I says awye til lat.

So I bounced from le taxi up til Mr Red White and Blue's flat an flung le door open an sure he was standin in le middle of le room, shirtless, his chest like a brick shithouse, his muscles flexin, an wih just lem chinos on. An I was gushin, like Niagara Falls. He was le biggest buck I'd ever seen. I went over til him an he led me straight til le red room of pain, shuttin le door behind us.

Nen he says til me, 'Now Margaret, you were a bad girl today. You must be punished. Strip.'

So I says, 'Yes, sir,' an tuck le lat off in about ten seconds. Nen he sat on le edge of le big bed an told me to lie face down on le bed. So I climbed on til le bed an shoved my baps in his face on le way past, but he just ignored lem, an I says til myself, oh here, he musta somethin special in store for me le night. So he starts to tie my hands an feet til le bed an I says til him, 'I wonder hie small people have a bondage buck, sure they wud be too small to stretch out on le bed.'

An he says til me, 'You just need a longer

rope.'

An I says til him, 'Please don't tell me you've been buckin dwarfs in lis bed.'

An he laughs an says, 'I don't talk about the past.'

An nen I knew lat he had. An I was a bit ragin an about to kick off wih him when he sets a pair a earphones on my head.

An here's me, 'Whaaaaaaaa?'

An lis is him, 'It's all about control, I want to control what you hear and feel.'

An I says, 'Have ye gat any Lady Gaga ler?'

But sure doesen he start playin some crazy opera music lat's like music to kill yerself til. An I was about to complain when I feels a massive slap til my arse, an what wih nat knowin it was comin, it was too much of a shack to really hurt. Nen he did it again an again an I started to know when ley were comin cos every time I heard le twat on le violin go beserk I gat a wallopin by Mr Red

White and Blue. An nen I started to count le slaps. An I think lis musta been turnin him on cos in between slaps he was strokin my arse an le Muff was gettin a tickle too. Nen, le music stapped an he untied me an sure we went for it like two maniacs all over le bed an le floor. We even had a wee go on le swing, but after bits of dust an cement started comin down from le ceiling, we moved off lat an back til le big bed.

Nen, after we were done, I was lyin on his chest an luckin at le scars on him an he says, 'Don't look at me, I can't stand it.'

Nen I tells him lat he's a big buck but he just smiles. Nen I says til him, 'So tell me, did ye play "Hi ho, hi ho, it's off to work we go," on le earphones for le dwarf when you were smackin le hole off hor?' Nen he just laughs an says it's time to go. Nen I says til him, 'Maybe we cud just stay here? Just for le night?' But I feels him tense up an I know it's a no, so I just gets dressed an leaves, an I can tell he's as annoyed as I am at his fucked-up-ness.

So I gets intil le flat to find Big Sally-Ann an Igor naked an havin a dirty ride up against my flat windee. I thought til myself, frig me, if he's nat doin it outside, he has to be luckin out le windee!

He's too busy goin at it to notice me, but Big Sally-Ann nods at me an says, 'I left ye half a beef chow mein in le microwave, chum.'

So I says, 'Thanks luv,' an saunters intil le kitchen to heat it up. When I gets back intil le livin room, ley are still goin strong, an Igor is shoutin, 'Zally-Ann, Zally-Ann!' An hor eyes are rollin in hor head as he's buckin hor further up le windee, so I just saunter on intil my bedroom to eat in ler an leave lem til it. Like, I was a bit worried lat le weight of le two a lem pushin against le windee wud crack it open an ley'd end up in le street, tatey bread. But sure ley were havin too much fun to interrupt lem for a health an safety talk. An nen again, Big Sally-Ann might want to get hor arm broke or somethin to get a claim cos she was torturin me about gettin le money up for a feg run. An le last time she'd needed a bidda cash quick, she'd run out on le road in front of a bin lorry an gat cuncusion from whackin hor head off le road. So I leaves lem til it an I sits on my bed an starts to wing le Chinese intil me.

Nen, I gets a text from Mr Red White and Blue lat says, 'I'm sorry for being like this. I will come and stay the night with you tomorrow, I promise.' An I was so excited I spat out le noodles in my mouth an yelled, 'Yesssss! Yesssss!' just as Big Sally-Ann next door was screamin, 'Yeesssss! Yesssss!'

15

An Ice-cream Poke

Well. Le next day sure I cud hardly contain myself wih thinkin about Mr Red White and Blue comin to stay le night wih me. I cudden cancentrate on Jeremy Kyle enough even to work out if le chavs were lyin or nat, an I always guess it right like. Big Sally-Ann an Igor had stayed le night on my sofa an I was woke up til him growlin an hor wailin an I knew ley were at it again. An sure I was a bit put out, like, cos ler was Igor only wih hor a few days an already spendin le night wih hor, an Mr Red White and Blue was only just thinkin about it nie. But sure, I thought til myself, better late lan never.

So, after Igor left, Big Sally-Ann an me had a bacon sandwich an a feg an I gat le lowdown on ler relationship. Sure she was in love wih him an he had said he loved hor too. Nen he had said he was probably gonna have to leave le country within weeks an sure Big Sally-Ann was gutted about lat. I was a bit worried about where it was gonna go myself cos sure I heard thon big lawd Stephen Nolan talkin on the radio about some eejit that had been fixin marriages to get his family intil Belfast. An when he run outta women to agree to be brides for him, he used to get le men to come here on haliday, buck needy women an nen propose to lem. Nen le women lat gat married were drapped as soon as le men gat in le country. So I was gonna have to keep my eye on le big girl, cos she was smitten like.

After she left, I tried to have a wee doze

but I cudden settle. I kept thinkin about Mr Red White and Blue in my bed an what he was gonna do til me. Nen, when I was wonderin hie I was gonna put le day in, sure didden I get a text from Sinead askin me did I wanna go down le town for a bidda shapliftin. So lis is me, awye til lat! So I met hor at le battam a North Street an we danders along til CastleCourt. Sinead was luckin some make up to sell on le internet so we went intil Debenhams. Sure lem tarts on le counter lucked at us like we were scumbegs an lat just made me wanna stale more.

So, we gat lis girl lat was about six foot tall, she had bright red lipstick on an had a pointy nose an big drew-on eyebrows. An I gat busy askin questions about le Dior sparkly lipgloss while Sinead started drappin stuff intil hor beg. Nie we knew ler were cameras ler but wee pros like us knew where le blind spats were. An le left side of le Dior counter was one of lem. So le girl on le till knew lis too an she kept luckin at le display stand to see what was missin like. So, I asked hor to do my face up an said I wud buy somethin like. So she starts wih le eyeshadow an le blusher an all an I thinks til myself, sure lis is great – free make-over for my night wih Mr Red White and Blue. An by le time she's finished, Sinead is chompin at le bit to get outta ler wih hor stash. So le girl on le till hands me a mirra an sure I lucked like somethin from le eighties. Black eyeshadow an eyeliner, orange blusher an red lipstick an here's me, 'Whaaaaaaa? I luck like a fuckin drag queen luv.'

An lis is hor, 'You said you wanted an evening look.'

An lis is me, 'Aye, I did. But nat an evenin wih Danny La Rue.'

An lis is hor, 'Well you said you'd buy something.'

An lis is me, 'You said you cud do make-up luv, I'm buyin nathin.'

So, she stood ler wih hor arms crossed an mumbled somethin til herself lat sounded like 'milly' so lis is me, I'm nat havin lat.

So, iss is me til hor, 'Here luv, I'm no friggin milly. You're standin ler like you own le bloody place. Nie ye did me up like a hooker – sure I cud make a fortune round at le Albert Clack the night!' Nen I sees Sinead stuffin a bax a bronzin balls intil her beg so I decides to take le hissy fit a bit further to let her nick some more. So I acts all hurt an offended an I says, 'You've no right to luck down on us, like. Sure you only work in a shap. A shap! Same as if I worked in a corner shap sellin fegs an 10p mix-up begs or a charity shap sellin cardigans lat smell a pish.'

Nen hor face goes bright red an sure I sees a crowd a people, mostly wimen shappers, luckin over an smilin, an I knew ley were thinkin le exact same as me. So I says, 'See ye. Wudden wanna be ye.' An links

Sinead's arm.

Nen Sinead says over hor shoulder, 'Ye have to be a whore to work at Dior.' An we strolls outta ler like we are two swanks.

Well. It was worth it all cos Sinead had done a blinder an nicked half a le stack. She had lipsticks, eyeliners, foundation, bronzin balls – le lat. Yer talkin five hundred quids worth, at least. So we sat on a wee wall out le back a CastleCourt an split le make-up in half so we both gat a good mix a stuff. We were pissin ourselves at yer woman on le till, nen Sinead says she had to go to get hor stash on le internet by dinner time. An I says til hor, 'We'll have to do lis again, chum.'

An lis is hor, 'Big time!' Nen she hugs me an danders up to get le bus home.

So, once I gat home, I had to get le clown face scrubbed off me an start gettin ready for Mr Red White and Blue. So, I painted my nails bright red an done my toenails too. I had to go next door an barrow Mrs Finlay's cheese grater for le hard skin on my feet cos they were like two pig's hoofs, like. Sure I had to tell hor it was parmesan I was gratin cos I cudden get le wee bits a skin outta it when I give hor it back. She wudden notice anyway sure she's blind in one eye. Nen, I tuck out an eyeliner an blusher from my Dior stuff an I piled it on. Sure I kept addin til it an I was a bit like Miss Piggy by le time le buzzer rang.

But sure Mr Red White and Blue kept til his word an ler he was, at my flat door to stay le night. I cud tell from le luck in his eye lat he had it in for me again an I was glad lat I had lubed my arse up wih baby oil just before he came. I thought lat maybe it wud make his big hand slide off my skin an maybe it wudden hurt as much gettin slapped. But sure when he came in wasn't he all calm an all. Lucked like he'd never walloped a woman in his life. He had a bunch of flowers for me an a battle a Paris Hilton 'Siren' perfume an here's me, 'Whaaaaaaa?' Nobady ever bought me flowers an perfume an I says til myself, oh here, he can have me anyway he wants me le night, sure I pure love him! But he says it was like an apalagy for psycho Deirdre's behaviour at le Bru.

Nen I says til him, 'Nie, is lat le last I'll hear from hor like?'

Nen he says, 'I really hope so, Margaret. But she does seem a bit on the edge, I'm keeping a close eye on her.'

Nen I says, 'Maybe I should send a gang down to give hor a fist sandwich an lat'll give hor le praper message.'

Nen he says, 'No, Margaret. I'll deal with her.'

Nen I says til him, 'What did y'ever see in thon hoor anyway? She's no diddies nor nathin. She's like a boy wih two backs.'

Nen he says, 'She reminds me of my birth mother, Margaret – all my subs do, even you.'

Nen I says til him, 'Here, I'm no sub – ye don't get me in a meal deal wih a Coke an a packet of crisps.'

Nen he says, 'No, Margaret, not a subway – a submissive. I was her master. Like the way I want to be your master.'

Nen I says, 'Awye, well I'm still thinkin about lat, chum.'

Nen he comes over til me an starts to kiss my neck an I say, 'So hie do I remind you of yer ma like?' An I know lis is a touchy subject so I am a bit stiff about askin him, like.

Nen he says, 'It's your accent. She talked like you.'

An here's me til myself, I dunno whether to take lis as a compliment or nat, like. But len doesen he start to lick my ears an all, an I go all giggly.

Nen he says, 'Margaret. I'd like to play with you. Get on the bed and strip naked.'

So here's me, 'Ye don't have til ask me

twice big lawd.'

So I runs intil le bedroom an he shouts in after me askin if I had any ice cream an I shouts back to check le freezer cos I hadn't a clue. So sure as I'm flingin my clothes aff, I hears him crashin about in le kitchen, bangin stuff an all. An I thinks til myself, what's he on about ice cream for? Sure I am gaggin for a bidda man-cream, like.

Nen sure he appears in le doorway wih a big tub a ice cream an a wooden spoon. He has lis wicked smile an he grabs my sacks from le floor an starts to tie my arms til le tap of my bed. Nen he lifts my bra an knickers up an ties my feet til le baddam a le bed wih lem. So I'm naked an spread like a starfish an I thinks til myself, nie ler's nathin straightforward about lis big lawd, ler always has to be somethin gettin tied up or what-have-ye. But sure I was dead excited too cos after seein Big Sally-Ann gettin bucked up against le windee, I was moist all day waitin for my turn.

So, once I was all tied up, he pulls out a balaclava from his back packet an here's me, 'Whaaaaaaa? No way, chum. Lat brings back bad memories of le nineties.' Nen he says it's nat for him. It's for me an he pulls it over my head le wrong way round so I can't see at all. Nen I says, 'Frig, am I lat ugly ye don't wanna luck at me when you're buckin me?'

Nen he says, 'No, Margaret. You are lovely, it's so you can't see what I'm doing. It's about control for me.'

So I says, 'Awye, will.' But I was thinkin til myself, just get on wih it wud ye.

Nen I hear him say, 'Oh,' like all disappointed, so I asks him what's wrong. Nen he says he didden realise le ice cream was mint choc-chip but it wud do seein as I was tied up an all already. So sure he lifts le balaclava up til my nose an puts a big dollop of ice cream intil my gob an I start munchin on it. Nen he draps a big clap of it intil my belly button an it was freezin cos I'd been on fire from le waist down since I seen his arse in lem chinos, like, so I let a yelp outta me. So it started meltin right away but I was more worried about le fluff, cos my belly button makes a wild lat a fluff an pus ever since I gat lat infection. Sure big Sally-Ann had pierced it wih a skewer off hor Ma's barbeque set last Twelfth an it had never been right since. But sure len I remembers lat le ice cream was green anyway, an he'd nat notice le pus if ler was any.

Nen sure doesen he start plasterin my baps in le ice cream an sure I'm squealin le house down cos it's so cold it's nippin my nips, but sure Mr Red White and Blue is just laughin, lovin every minute of it. Nen he starts to slowly lick it off an sure I was ringin like Quasimodo's bell. He was takin his time, like, an I was gaggin for it – I was about to tell him to hurry up sure when he shoves a load of it on my fan-bax. Sure I lets out a 'Whoooooooooo!' an before I cud say anythin else, he was down ler eatin it aff.

An I says til him, 'Nie, lat's what I call a knicker-bucker glory' an le next thing I know, he's ridin me intil le night and, while I was lovin it, I was thinkin til myself, where le hell are lem chocolate chips gonna end up lat's gettin rammed up my quim?

So, after we'd finished, he untied me an we lay on le bed, kissin an talkin. He started talkin about his rattan birth ma who had abused him when he was wee – lat's why he had lem scars an all, an I thought, frig, he's openin up til me nie. Maybe we will be a normal couple one day an go to Ikea an buy candles an salad bowls. Nen sure didden I fall asleep in his arms an I dreamt I was Cinderella an Mr Red White and Blue was Prince Charmin.

Le next mornin, I woke up singin, 'One

day, my prince will come,' an I felt like a right dick. So I thinks til myself, right, I'm gonna surprise Mr Red White and Blue an wake him up wih a blowie to make him wanna stay over more often. But sure when I flung le sheets back, his dick was manky like it had some weird infection.

So I started screamin an he jumped up yellin, 'What? What? What's wrong?'

Nen I says, 'Luck at your knob, chum. It's dead.' An he lucks down at it an it's all green skebs an black spats an all, an sure he busts out laughin!

An here bes him, 'It's okay Margaret. It's just the ice cream. Mint choc-chip? Green? I didn't wash it off last night.'

Nen I says, 'Frig me. Lat's what I call a spatted dick like.' Nen sure he grabs me, flings me on le bed an has his wicked way wih me again before he has to go to work.

Nen after he goes, I lay in bed an smoked ten fegs one after le orr an daydreamed about my weddin reception in le Rex bar an all. But len I gat a phone call from le Bru an was told I'd to go down for a back-til-work interview le next day, an I knew right away lat hoor Deirdre was on my case again. So I gat dressed an went to find Big Sally-Ann to discuss hie we were gonna deal wih le bitch, an to tell hor about le ice-cream buck. Sure I was pissin lem choc-chips out for le rest of le week, so I swore til myself lat was le last time I wud get bucked wih mint choc-chip ice cream in my Mary.

16

Maggie's Mix Tape

Well. Big Sally-Ann was fit to be tied when I told hor about thon hoor from le Bru gettin me in le shit again. We were round in my flat plannin what to do an she wanted to go an wait for hor after work an empty hor outside, but I says no til lat cos she wud get us tuck off le Bru. It was a tricky situation, like. So, I ended up tellin hor all about le mint-choc-chip ice cream sex instead an sure she said she was away out to get some for Igor cos he wud like lat, an it wud stap him wantin sex in bushes an lay-bys an all. So after she went, I was sittin eatin gravy rings, watchin

Loose Women, when I heard a rap at le door. So I opens it an ler is a courier ler wih a wee package for me.

An lis is him, 'Special delivery – you need to sign for it.' An lis is me til myself, oh my God, it's from Mr Red White and Blue – maybe it's a diamond from Lunns! So, I ripped it open an sure wasn't it one a lem wee iPod shuffle things to listen til music til. I'd seen wee lawds down at le Bru wih lem in ler ears wih rave music blastin out.

Well, sure I gets settled on le sofa an reads le wee card an it says, '*I hope this says everything I can't.*' So, I turns it on an sure hassen le wee romantic made me a modern-day mix tape. An sure I was fourteen again. Wee Mikey Wright had made me a mix tape at Christmas lat year wih East 17's 'Stay' on it. I was so chuffed, I tuck his cherry at le back of le kebab shap on le Road. But lis was different. Sure I turned it on an it was all lis opera music lat he had smacked my arse til.

An lis is me, nie lat's nat my idea of relaxin, rememberin gettin my melt knacked in. Plus, if anybody on le Road heard me listenin til lat tripe, my street cred wud be ruined forever. An it's tuck me years to build lat up too.

So, I decided to show le big lawd hie it's done an gat to makin him a praper mix tape on a CD cos I didden know hie to work le shuffle hing. So, here is le songs I put on it.

1) Britney Spears – 'Hit Me Baby One More Time'
2) Michael Jackson – 'Beat It'
3) R.E.M. – 'Everybody Hurts'
4) Guns N' Roses – 'Pretty Tied Up'
5) Ian Dury – 'Hit Me With Your Rhythm Stick'
6) Culture Club – 'Do You Really Want To Hurt Me'
7) Prodigy – 'Smack My Bitch Up'

8) Rihanna – 'Disturbia'
9) Lady Gaga – 'Bad Romance'
10) Take That – 'Why Can't I Wake Up
   With You'

An sure I was dead pleased wih myself. But sure listenin til all lem songs made me wanna get a wallopin again so sure I texts Mr Red White and Blue, 'Thanks for le i-shuffle thing. I made you a CD too, I'll bring it round le night.'

Nen he texts back, 'Nice one. See you later babe.' Nen sure I was dancin about like a giddy twit cos he called me babe.

So, later lat night, I gat til his flat an sure didden he have le snooker table set up for us to have a game.

An I says til him, 'Nie ye do know I'm a hustler like.'

An he just smiles an says, 'We'll see. I never lose, Margaret. At anything.'

Nen I thinks til myself, ye lost yer marbles

chum when you started buckin thon Mrs Robinson, but sure I never said nathin cos I cud see he was in a good mood.

So, len, he tuck le CD an put it on. Le first song started to belt out, 'Hit Me Baby One More Time' an sure he laughs an says til me, 'Very funny. Are they all like lis?' An I laugh an lift le snooker cue an break le balls up on le table.

Nen he says til me, 'Now Margaret, if you are being cheeky, you know I will have to punish you.' An nen I bites my lip on purpose an passes him le cue. So, he patts a couple of balls an I thinks til myself, frig he is good, like, but sure I was determined nat to let him win. So I goes to take my shot an I leans over le table to line it up when he comes up behind me an pushes me intil le table wih his stiffy.

An lis is me, 'You tryin to distract me big lawd?' An he starts kissin my ear. Nen I say, 'I'll have ye know, I won le pool room tournament four years in a row when I used to go ler.'

Nen he says, 'I bet you did. I'm sure the guys couldn't take their eyes off you bending over the table like this. Tell me, did you wear a short skirt like this?' An sure he pulls my skirt up over my arse cheeks til it's round my waist an says, 'What a lovely round ass you have.' An sure he starts squeezin my cheeks. An I just smiled an thought, cancentrate, cancentrate.

But sure as I goes to pat le ball, he hooks a finger round my thong an pulls it down til my knees. Nen he hits me such a slap. So I pretend to ignore it an takes le shot an I pat le ball, just as I get another smack. Nen, I feel his big tripod tryin to find le Muff from behind.

An I says til him, 'Here mate, make sure you pat le pink ler an nat le brown like.'

Nen he whispers intil my ear, 'I'll pot le brown another day.' An I thinks til myself, never in a month of Sundays, chum.

Nen he says, 'You need to take another shot.' So I goes to take le shot an sure his hand comes down on my backside again an nen he starts pummellin me from behind an I miss le ball. But sure as I'm gettin bucked over le table, I take advantage of le situation an move a few a his balls on le table round an snooker le cont.

So, by le time 'Smack My Bitch Up' is blarin outta le stereo, sure he has me lyin on le snooker table on my back wih my skirt round my waist an my tap pulled up. My legs were up his front an over his shoulders an he was holdin me down wih le snooker cue. Nen, after we were finished, he says til me, 'I think we'll have to abandon this game, Margaret.'

An I says, 'Awye. Ye were losin anyway.' Nen he tells me we are gonna take a shawer together an I says awye til lat. So, we trats intil le bathroom an sure doesen he grab me an trail me intil le shawer wih my clothes still on! An sure I was laughin my head off as he turned on le water.

Nen he says til me, 'Touch me, Margaret.'

An I thinks til myself, oh frig, he's never let me touch his scars nor nathin. So, I carefully peeled off his shirt lat was stuck til him by len wih le water an sure he's all right wih it. An nen I thinks til myself, frig, he must love me a wee bit. Nen he pulls my tap off over my head an I take my bra off an release le baps. Nen he starts soapin my baps up wih a sponge an I have a wee tickle of his middle leg. Nen he goes to take my denim skirt off an sure it's stuck til me wih le water. He yanks it, pulls it, twists it an it's nat for movin. So in le end, I had to lie on le floor wih my feet against le toilet while he stood over me an trailed it off me. Lis is me til myself, I need to go on a serious diet like. Nen sure he lets me wash him too an I thinks I might be in heaven. It reminded me of le time Jack painted Rose on le *Titanic*, luckin at each others bits but nat buckin, like. So, after lat, we puts our clothes on le radiator to dry an goes intil le bedroom. Nen sure doesen he have me again on le bed. An no whips, chains, nathin lis time. Nen I fell asleep in his arms.

17

Deirdre Goes Ape-shit

Well. Le next mornin, it was le day of my back-til-work interview wih le wee cont Deirdre at le Bru. So Mr Red White and Blue left for work first an sure he says til me to have some breakfast an to saunter on down til le Bru when I was ready. So I gat a cuppa tea an a feg an sure I decided to take a luck around his flat. I was takin a nosey in his wardrobe an I sees lis black bax down at le battam, so I lifts it out an carries it on til le bed. Well, sure wasn't it full of details of his past subs. Ler pictures, ler dress an bra sizes, ler cantracts, everythin. So I picks up one of le pictures an right enough, it was a wee dwarf woman. An I wonder if he patted hor brown on le snooker table. An sure I was ragin wih jealousy.

One of le women was like a madal – all cheek bones an eyelashes an sure I was like a batein bear, so I was, imaginin hor an MY Mr Red White and Blue havin a bath tilgether, or in le red room of pain. An nen another picture was of a wee square-luckin woman an I thinks til myself, feck he's nat choosey like is he? Lat's like goin from Pamela Anderson til Deirdre Barlow! Sure she had a bake on hor like a full skip. It wudda turned milk. Nen, I lucked a bit closer an sure I near had a fit – It was Deirdre-pancake-diddies from le Bru! Sure ye cudden mistake lem thin lips an mousey brown hair hangin off hor head like le end of a mop. So, I shoved all le pictures back intil le bax an went to get dressed. I was in two minds whether or nat to take le pictures down til le backyard an set lem on fire but len Mr Red White and Blue wud know I was noseyin about his flat an I didden want lat. Even though I was ragin lat he had kept all lem pictures an details of his ex-subs.

But sure little did I know, more drama was til come. Sure I tried to get my clothes on an ley had shrunk wih hangin over le radiator all night. My white belly tap was just about coverin my baps an my denim skirt just about went on, but it wudden zip up. An for le life of me, I cudden find my knickers anywhere. I was gonna put somethin on belongin til Mr Red White and Blue but all he had was suits an ties an all lat shite. So I left le flat an headed til le Bru wih my red bra pokin out below my shrunken tap, an le Muff hangin outta le gap in my denim skirt lat wudden zip up. I was like a big hoor. So, after about fifty cars beepin me an women tuttin at me, I finally arrived at le Bru. I tucked what pubes I cud back intil my skirt an sat down. Nen, out came dozy Deirdre wih hor cordyroy skirt flappin down til hor ankles an hor bowl haircut. An sure she is pure harrified at me wih all my bits on show. Sure doesen she lose le bap an takes a run at me wih a stapler. She was tryin to staple my head when le security guard an a couple of le orr staff pulled hor off me. Sure she had to get restrained in le middle of le Bru an all le wee lawds in le dole queue were cheerin an all.

So, sure le manager of le Bru came out til me an is all apalagisin til me sayin he didden know what had come over hor an was askin me was I gonna put a claim in an all. Nen I says lat I wudden put a claim in if I didden have to go back ler for any more back-til-work interviews, on account of it bein too traumatic for me goin back til le scene of le attack an all. So, he says awye til lat an I thinks til myself, result!

Nen, as I was walkin out, sure I sees Mr Red White and Blue talkin til Deirdre an holdin hor hand an sure I was fumin. But sure I cudden say nathin cos he's nat allowed to buck any dolers an he'd get sacked if he did. So I had to walk out an leave lem an I was pure ragin.

But nen, on le way up home, wee Winky Moore, le taxi driver from le Road, stapped to give me a lift, an to add insult til injury, sure le wee frigger tried it on wih me. An ye wanna seen him – he's a pure munter! His teeth's like knit one skip one an he's about sixty.

Lis is him til me, 'Whaddabout a lumber in le back seat an a free fare?'

An lis is me, 'Ack away an buck a duck ye dirty baste – sure ye haven't a bar in yer grate!' An nen I flings a fiver at him an scoots outta le taxi.

Nen as I let myself intil le flat, I thought about Mr Red White and Blue's teeth. All straight wih none missin an just lovely – when ley are nat bitin my baps lat is. An I lay

on my bed an remembered le snooker table
sex an all an sure I was soakin. Nen I thinks
til myself, hie can I make Mr Red White and
Blue fall in love wih me? What do I have to
do? Nen it hits me. I have to let him be my
master. Call him 'sir' when he's wallopin me,
let him do what he wants til me in his red
room of pain an maybe, just maybe, take a
luck at lat cantract again. Nen I says til myself,
right, I'm gonna get my sexiest clothes on an
you know what? Le Muff is goin. I'm gonna
shave le beast off once an for all for Mr Red
White and Blue so off I trat to le bathroom
to dickey myself up, chantin, 'No muff too
tough, no muff too tough.'

18

No Pain, No Gain?

Well. Sure wasn't my Gilette razor like a rusted door hinge, it'd been lat long since I'd used it. So sure didden I hack at le muff like I was de-weedin le garden an ended up wih a fanny lat lucked like a game of noughts an crosses – wee stubborn hairs stickin up in all directions. Ye cudda laid me down an used me as a stinger to catch joyriders on le Westlink. But sure lat's what Mr Red White and Blue wanted an lat's what he wud get. So I picks out a leopard print boob tube lat Big Billy Scriven said my baps lucked lush in, an a red leather miniskirt lat I gat in Benidorm

128

on le feg run. An I finished off le luck wih a pair a gold hoop earrings an red stillettos. Sure a lucked in le mirra at myself an here's me 'I'd buck ye, ye cert ye.' So off I went, no kacks on nor nathin, pure buck material like.

Nen I gets til his flat an rung le buzzer an sure his voice is all sad, he says, 'Hi.'

An I says, 'It's Bell big lawd. An my knickers aren't ringin cos I have none on!'

An nen I hears him heavy breathin down le intercom an here's me til myself, oh here, I'm in for it nie. So I runs up to le flat an sure he near bates le door down to get til me an lumbers le bake off me in le doorway.

Nen I says, 'I missed ye, like.'

Nen he says, 'Me too, Margaret.'

Nen sure I takes a pure beamer! Redner or whaaaaaaa? So I says til him, 'Right big lawd. Forget what happened le day at le Bru an I never wanna hear yer woman's name mentioned again. Nie, do what ye want til me – I am still nat signin no cantract nor nathin but if I shout, 'Ulster says NO!' ye have to stap, right?'

Nen he says okay til lat, so I runs intil le bedroom, jumps on le bed an hitches my skirt up to show off my butchered Mary an I says, 'Nie get yer chaps round lat chum.'

Nen he sees my banjaxed shavin job I done an sure he goes intil one. He whips aff his chinos in a oner an takes a run at me like he's about to dive-bomb at le swimmers.

Well. Molestin isn't le word. I was bucked, screwed, chewed an stripped nude an sure wasn't I lovin it! He flung me lis way an lat, had me hangin off le bed wih le blood rushin til my head an nen he flips me over an has me from le back an sure I was like a rag doll. Every position in le *Kama Sutra* was done.

Nen he says for me to go over til lis big wooden bar thing so I goes an he puts my head an my hands through three holes in it so I'm hangin like I'm about til get my head chapped off or somethin. Nen he puts lat blindfold on me again an I says til myself, Lord what's he up til nie. Nen sure I gets ready for a whip or a smack but sure doesen he belt me wih somethin lat feels like a stick an I scream, 'Jeysus, Mary an Joseph, what le fuck was lat?' It was achin.

An he says, 'Call me sir!'

Nen I say, 'What le fuck was lat, sir?'

Nen he tells me to shut up an here's me til myself, here, I'm nat havin lis like. So I'm about to tell him nat to talk to me like lat when he wallops le breath outta me wih le stick thing an here's me 'Whaaaaaaaaaaaaaaaa!' an he starts comin down on my arse wih le stick over an over an I cud hardly breathe wih le pain. Hanast ta God it was like gettin stabbed in le arse wih a pitchfork by a big farmer.

Nen I remembers le safe word an I shouts, 'Ulster says NO!' But sure le bastard kept on hittin me an my arse was on fire. An nen le rage built up in me an I was goin ballistic screamin, 'Get me out ye bastard!' I was wrigglin an tryin to pull my head outta le trap I was in an I was thinkin til myself, he's gonna get emptied when I get outta here. An nen he musta snapped outta le frenzy cos he stapped an he drapped le stick an was sayin sarry over an over an I says, 'Get me le fuck outta lis thing nie!' An nen when he finally released me, I jumped up, I was even cryin wih rage, an I turned round an stuck le head intil le cont. An here's me, 'Belfast kiss ye ballbeg!' He stumbled backwards an fell on le bed, holdin his snout.

Nen I says, 'You fucked up Disturbia cont ye.' An he tries to say sarry an asks me do I want some Sudocrem for my arse an I says, 'Naaaaa. But your gonna need your nose lucked at.' Sure le blood was pissin outta it – it lucked like a busted boot. Nen I grabs my clothes, shoves lem on an leaves him standin ler.

An I walks outta his flat thinkin, no man's gonna bate le life outta me no matter hie gorgiz he is in lem chinos. I'm nat havin it, I'm a friggin goddess, I'm every woman, it's all in me! Girl parrr! So I think til myself, next stap, le boney. Sally-Ann'll cheer me up a treat. An wih only one night left til le Eleventh Night, we had to pratect it from gettin burnt down again. So I danders intil le estate an ler she is, sittin in le middle of a crowd of wee lads, tellin lem all about hor fire-fightin skills. An nen she sees me an comes over. Sure I near dies tellin hor about lat brute canin me, an she says, 'Nie lat's a bit too far, like. Nathin wrong wih a bidda bondage – sure I drapped candle wax on Jimmy Long's bell-end an put a tennis ball in his mouth an he loved it – sure, he ended up wih lack-jaw, like, but said it was worth it.'

Nen I tells hor about me stickin le head intil him an all an she says til me, 'Oh yer a pure geg Maggie, no wonder ye lamped him! Beezer!'

Nen I realises lat I don't need a man anyways, sure I have my Big Sally-Ann. An chums are thicker lan water. So I asks hor about Igor an she says til me, 'Ack, sure didden he get lifted last night for exposin himself til le public?'

An here's me, 'Whaaaaaaaa?'

An lis is hor, 'Awye. Sure we were havin a quickie up against a tree in le back a le Grove Park an sure two peelers were walkin by le railins an saw us at it. So, we bolted an sure, I flew intil Brantwood an hid in le toilets but he run le orr way an ley caught him.' So I has to laugh like.

Nen she says, 'Sure, it's better til be single over le Twelfth anyhie, so ye can buck who ye want to, like.'

An nen lis is me, 'True, like.'

Nen we saunters over til le wee lads at le boney an ley all make room for me an Sally-Ann to sit down.

An she winks at me an says, 'I beggsey him wih le Kappa tap on an his mate wih le vest tap for afters.'

Nen I lucks at le rest a lem an says, 'Fuck it, 'mon we'll get intil le hut in le boney an have a gang bang!' So we grabbed le blue begs full of Bucky an glue an run intil le middle of le boney, laughin our balls aff.

19

Maggie's Twelfth

Well. It all started on le Eleventh Night. Big Sally-Ann was on a pramise wih wee Jason Bailie from le Shankill Road Defenders Band. But sure didden he think it was 1994 again an turned up til le boney in one of lem Celtic taps, thinkin it wud be a pure geg. But sure didden he get his melt knacked in by lem two hoors, Nikki an Kelly from Glencairn. Baseball bats an everyhin. Lem two cud be bouncers at Drumcree so they cud. So Big Sally-Ann was ragin an tried it on wih wee Corey Murphy. Like, he's only sixteen an his ma hit le roof an wallaped hor over le napper wih a big battle a blue WKD an nen sure wasn't ler blue murder.

I jumped in an smacked le bake off hor, an nen hor chum Davina (thon singer from le Road wih le monobrow) shoved me til le ground an sure didden I land on a bidda broken glass an it cut le arse off me. An all lat was before le boney was even lit! So sure didden we end up havin to get a taxi up til le Mater. Sally-Ann gat hor head stitched an I gat my arse stitched. An sure le wee nurse, Natalie, musta seen all le bruises on my arse from my whippin from Mr Red White and Blue cos sure on le way out she handed me a leaflet on 'domestic violence'.

But sure I just laughed an says til hor, 'Ack, luv, it's all right. It was a man from le Bru done lat in his red room of pain an sure he ended up wih a nose like a busted soda.' An nen sure didden she back away from me like I was crawlin wih crabs or somethin.

But Big Sally-Ann was dyin to get back til le boney to see if she cud get a ride.

Here she is til me, 'If I don't get my hole le night it'll rain le marra, lat always happens. 2004 til 2006 when I was in Maghaberry sure it rained every Twelfth.'

Nen I says, 'Frig Sally-Ann are ye sayin ye can predict le weather by your fanny like? They shud have ye on doin le weather on UTV – get boned by wee Frank on air every day an sure Belfast will be like Benidorm wih sunshine!'

So sure we gets a taxi back til le Road an le boney's lit an all. Every cont's paired off wih somebady an ler's nat a buck in sight. Even Billy Scriven's snoggin le bake off Big Ellen 'Le Dungeon' Donnan up against le railins an gropin le diddies off hor. She was takin a drag of hor feg in between lumbers an sure I was ragin! Nen sure me an Sally-Ann saw lem goin for a quickie in Asda carpark an I says til hor, ''Mon, we'll nick ler carry-out.'

So we snuck over til le railins an Big Sally-Ann grabbed le blue beg. I lucked over le railins as he was tryin to shove his wee acorn up hor arse an I says til myself, Ack fair play til lem.

So we runs down le road wih le blue beg an sure it was like Christmas. I put my hand in an pulled out a battle a Bucky an Big Sally-Ann put hor hand in an pulled out a battle of Pernod. We downed le lat so our Eleventh Night wudden be spoilt an decided to walk til le taxi rank an go over til le East.

I says, 'Sure we've bucked all le men over here anyway, 'mon we'll go where nobady knows us an get some fresh sausage.'

Nen Big Sally-Ann says, 'I'm hopin for a Cumberland!'

Nen Big Ricky Mason passes us on his motorbike an sure we shouts at him to stap cos it's a matter of buck or death an sure we pramises him a blowie if he takes us til le East so he says, 'Awye, will.' So we all jumps on an le bike goes about a mile a decade wih le weight of Big Sally-Ann's arse an my baps.

So by le time we arrives at le biggest boney in le East, we are poleaxed an sure it's just gettin lit. Big Sally-Ann sorted Ricky out wih what he was owed for le lift while I readjusted my thong. Sure I had slid about on le back a thon bike lat much lat I'd ended up wih a muff wedgie. Sure an auld fanny floss is all right nie an again like, it clears out le cobwebs. An sure I hadn't had any action since I drapped Mr Red White and Blue.

So we walks over til le boney an le air is full a horn wih everybody eyein each orr up. Nen we sees two wee lads sittin on a crate a Special Brew an I says til Big Sally-Ann, 'Ler's two certs ler, an free drink too.' So we saunters over til lem an says 'Hiyas'. An sure we cudden believe our luck. They were Scatchies. Struck gold. So we sits down an starts gettin intil ler Special an nen sure about five minutes later we're snoggin le bakes off each orr.

So sure didden we end up in le Bellvar. It was a lack-in an a pound a pint. I think it musta been out-of-date cos ler were people throwin up all over le place but sure we drunk it anyway. Nen we danced til 'You're a Superstar' – Big Sally-Ann was spinnin hor wee lawd round le place an he was a bit green luckin an I was gropin mine under le table. He was a buck an a half like. Lovely an tall, wide shoulders an gorgiz twinkly eyes – an lat accent! Sure I was drippin.

Nen I says til him, "Mon back til my flat an I'll pull your tail for real.'

An he says he cudden cos he had to go back to check in wih his band – they were on a curfew. Nen I was about to smack le lips on him again when le lights went on an le music stapped.

We all lucked at le DJ like he was a ballbeg an he shouts on his mic, 'No buckin on le

141

dancefloor, luv!'

An nen sure I lucks on til le dancefloor an Big Sally-Ann's on tap a hor Scatchie ridin him like a cowgirl, an singin 'Le Sash'. An sure he's passed out on le floor an knows nathin a what she's doin til him. So we ends up gettin threw out an can't get a taxi or nathin. So we finds two big tyres off a tractor lat didden get burnt an roll lem intil McDanalds car park an lie in lem wih our arses in le hole an our arms an legs hangin out over le sides til we passed out wih le drink.

But sure didden we wake up to hear le bands playin in le distance an I knew it was le Twelfth! An sure I lucks to Big Sally-Ann an she's still uncancious. An ler's a big seagull sittin on hor thigh.

An here's me, 'Oi, kipper knickers, ler's a seagull wantin a feed of yer ham wallet here.'

An sure she jumps up an le bird flies away squawkin like an eejit. So we gets up an realise its eight a'clack an we've to be at

Carlisle Circus for nine. So we runs down to get a taxi like two batein bears. Big Sally-Ann walks in le lodge an lis year she was behind Pride a le Shore an she was ragin cos she'd already bucked lem all before.

So we gat til my flat an gat changed – no time for a shawer nor nathin. Big Sally-Ann plastered herself in Britney's 'Hidden Fantasy' perfume an I says til hor, 'Frig ler was nathin hidden about your fantasy last night – half of East Belfast saw your growler wrapped round lat Scatchie's pole on le dancefloor!'

An she says, 'Sure he drapped a trip intil my drink an I thought I was on a bed of rose petals wih Janny Depp.'

Nen we gets dressed an saunters out to hitch a lift wih somebady. I had said til le Scatchies we'd meet lem at le Field an have a 'touchy-feely-no-putty-inny' in le bushes an they says awye til lat.

So sure didden I walk beside Sally-Ann's

lodge an sure I was gettin eyed up by all le Pride a le Shore bandmen. I had on my Union Jack dress lat was tight in all le right places an my baps were near hangin outta it. An I had spray painted my hair red, white an blue too. An red, white an blue knickers. An sure none a le bandmen believed me about lat so every time we stapped for a pish stap, I had to show lem my kacks again. But I didden mind like. I says til lem, 'Who wants to play "Le Sash" on my gash le night?' But ler were no takers.

Nen sure after about an hour of walkin, didden le hangover kick in, an Big Sally-Ann wasn't allowed to drink til she gat til le field. Nen, me bein hor best chum an all, I said I'd nat drink til we gat ler either. So I cudden even have a hair of le dog nor nathin. But sure len I saw big Sandy le burger man – he sits outside le Kremlin every Saturday night makin cheeseburgers for le regulars an ler feg hegs (lat's me). So

I strolls up an gets a dirty cheeseburger to soak up some a le alcohol fumes.

So I'm standin ler hoofin it intil me an I hears lis voice behind me sayin, 'Whaddabout a bite of my hatdog luv?'

An I turns round an sure it's Big Billy Scriven standin gawkin at me. An lis is me, 'Hatdog? Jellybean more like.' Nen I strolls aff. An I thinks til myself, naaaaaaa. I think it's time I gat a new buck buddy, an one lat touches le sides instead a toothpick gettin shoved up a spout. Nen I catches back up wih Big Sally-Ann an we marches on til le field.

So sure didden we get til le field hars later an sure wasn't my ankles an heels cut to shreds wih my pink neon high heels. Big Sally-Ann had wore hor da's gutties lat he wears in le bakery an nen changed at le field inde silver platforms an I wished I had done le same.

Nen sure we was standin waitin on a

dirty big cheeseburger an I sees my Scatchie walkin past, linkin arms wih some hoor! Here's me 'Oiiiiiii, dirty dick! What you playin at?'

An he tries to run away but I callars him, grabbin him by le scruff, here's me, 'Yer on a pramise to me, ye cont ye.'

Nen he says, 'Let me go!' an sure doesen his girl tramp over an I lucks at hor an she's all long blonde hair an red lipstick.

An I says, 'Here fuck aff, luv. He's mine.' Nen she opens hor mouth to say somehin an sure I shoves my fist intil it before she can. Nen she staggers backward an starts cryin. An here's me, 'Ack where's she from? Malone Road or what?' An nen my Scatchie puts his arm around hor an walks off an I thinks til myself, plenty more fish in le sea, plenty more flies round le shite.

So me an Big Sally-Ann wolfs our burgers intil us an sits down on le grass to down what's left of our carryouts. I gat four battles of peach Concord an Big Sally-Ann gat two flasks of Pernod. So we were rightly like.

Nen we says, right, 'mon we'll go an find a buck. So sure didden big Sally-Ann bump intil hor Scatchie an away ley went intil le bushes an sure I was left on my own. Nen I sees lis man dancin on his own til le music from le poke van and, although I was seein double an cudden stand up straight, I thought he was all right luckin. So I saunters over til him an starts dancin wih him. An he's twirlin me round like my Uncle Marty does at weddins an I notices he has a beard lat's white an I says, ack I must be seein things cos his eyes are lovely, he's nat lat auld. So len sure I tells him about le bushes an I has to explain til him what a 'touchy-feely-no-putty-inny' is an he says it sounds like great fun, so off we trats til le bushes. We passed Big Sally-Ann who was on hor knees in front of hor Scatchie an says 'Hiyas,' nen we stapped a bit after hor.

An sure I says, 'Fuck it, 'mon we'll go le whole way.'

So sure doesen I whip my Union Jack dress up an fling off my kacks an he says til me, 'What happened to your fanny, luv?'

An I says til him, 'Long story, nie get to work on it, luv.' So he starts munchin an I'm standin against a tree luckin up at le leaves an thinkin til myself, frig I love le Twelfth!

Nen I lucks over an sees Big Sally-Ann standin against another tree an we smiles til each orr an she gives me a thumbs-up. Nen I says til yer man, 'Lie down chum, an get yer begs aff.' So he does what he's told an sure I thought I saw Moses sandals gettin flung off an I says, naaaaaa, I'm seein things. So sure his dick's standin up like a tent pole so I jumps on an does a bit a space-hoppin on le wee lad. An sure I gets carried away rollin my head around an moanin an wailin an flingin my arms around me an sure ages has passed. Nen Big Sally-Ann comes over an gives me a high-five an I'm still goin for it on le wee lad, nen she says, 'Oh fuck! Maggie, STAP!!'

An I staps an turns round an says, 'It's all right, I'm near finished, we'll get another burger in a minute chum.'

Nen she says, 'No, Maggie, stap! He's friggin dead!'

Nen I lucks down at him an sure wih all le adrenalin an all, I'm near sober again an she's right, le fucker has croaked it mid-buck. An I jumps off an shouts, 'Oh here, he musta had rigamortis in his dick cos I've been ridin him for ages!' Nen we runs til le St John's ambulance an tells lem an ley run intil le bushes an get him on a stretcher, an sure he's like a dead fly but has a big smile on his face. An I lucks at him an sure isn't he about ninety. Like an auld lad. Sittin on his belly is his brown Moses sandals an he still had his sacks on. Quality. So sure I says til him as he was carried past us til le ambulance, 'Out wih a bang chum, best way to go.'

Nen Big Sally-Ann's Scatchie brings us over whisky neat for le shack, an we sits at le edge a le bushes drinkin it an I feels it warmin up my cackles an I feels so in love wih my chum Big Sally-Ann an le wee Scatchie for helpin me an sure I says til lem, 'What about a game a "hide la sausage" in le bushes?'

An le wee Scatchie lucks at Big Sally-Ann an she says til him, 'I will if you will.'

An he says, 'Thought you'd never ask!' So we runs intil le bushes, flingin our kacks off as we go.

Acknowledgements

I would like to thank Blackstaff Press for publishing the book. Thanks to Maureen Boyle, my Open University tutor, who helped give me the confidence to show my writing to others. Thanks to Chrissie Manby, author, who gave me excellent advice on publishing and writing. Thanks to Sarah who met me at Waterstones coffee shop and kept me company on her lunch hour while I scribbled Maggie's shenanigans. Thanks to the chums that I bounced ideas off: Linda, Sam, Ricky, Jen, Trish, Ali, Julie, Roxy, Jules, Dean, Dawn, Anthony. Thanks to Reuben for the pictures for my Facebook page. Thanks to my mum for an honest opinion and excessive baby-sitting duties.

Finally, a gigantic thank you to all my Facebook fans – you have made my dream come true and I thank every single one of you for all the lovely comments and support. I hope that you enjoy the story.

Leesa. x